Escaping Ryan

Genoa Mafia Series Book II

By Ginger Ring

Escaping Ryan

Copyright © 2018 by Ginger Ring.
All rights reserved.
Second Print Edition: September 2018

Limitless Publishing, LLC
Kailua, HI 96734
www.limitlesspublishing.com

Formatting: Limitless Publishing

ISBN-13: 978-1-64034-974-2

Prologue

The Visitor

The kid who'd been paid to remove the lightbulb as a prank had done well. A trailer at the edge of the woods was the target. Tracy Martin lived there. Who would think such a weak mannered girl would be a threat? Clouds in the late night sky made the home even harder to see. The person inside would soon be out like the light also. It was a message. They needed to stay out of the territory.

Despite being careful, footsteps still made the old wood deck creak and moan. Raising a black gloved hand, the visitor knocked on the door. Applause from some game show on a television could be heard through the thin walls. It suddenly stopped, the person inside either turning it off or just lowering the volume. Stomps signaled someone was approaching.

The front door opened. "Hi, come on in," the young woman greeted, and pushed the screen door wide so they could step inside.

She turned her back and the visitor followed.

"I've been looking forward to this all day." The woman slipped on a pair of high heels. "Do you want a drink before we go?"

"Sure, why not." Her invited guest shut the door and quietly locked it as Tracy grabbed a bottle from a kitchen cabinet near the sink. The house had an open floorplan with the kitchen, dining room, and living room all in one. A very small space where moving boxes littered the floor.

"How long have you been here?"

"A couple months." She motioned to the mess. "But with work and everything, I just haven't had a chance." Her outreached hand held a drink. "Wow, you're wearing gloves already?"

"I haven't gotten used to the cold yet." The drink was now in hand but soon set on the counter.

"It's crazy how you adapt to the weather. In spring, it hits thirty-two degrees and we think it's a heatwave. It drops to fifty in the fall and we have the gloves and coats on."

"Yes. So are you ready to go?"

Tracy took a sip from her glass. "I thought you wanted a drink."

"I changed my mind. Since I'm driving, I'd better not risk it."

She shrugged her shoulders. "Probably a good idea." Tracy set her glass on the counter. "Let me get a jacket." She turned and her visitor struck. The prick of a needle hit the side of Tracy's neck.

"Ouch." Her hand reached for the spot and was met by a syringe held by a gloved hand. "What the...? What are you doing?" she screamed, her mind not comprehending what was happening. The attacker wouldn't let go until all of the drug was in. It was very powerful, so not much was needed.

Tracy panicked. The fight or flight response kicked in. With labored breaths she fought back. With all her might she pushed back and shoved her assailant up against the counter and they grunted in pain. It was a brief victory.

Tracy shivered as her body quickly chilled. She was nauseous. Whatever was in the needle was now flowing through her system with a vengeance. Her fingers shook. The room swam. Her assailant released her, but what good was it now. There was no victory to be had. The damage had been done. But why? Tears flowed from her eyes. Tracy staggered to the dining room table and slowly turned around.

"What are you doing?" Her mouth felt like cotton. Her vision blurred.

"You took something that I wanted." The voice was unhuman.

"What?" Her fading consciousness wrangled with why this was happening but no ideas came to mind. Suddenly, the room went black. She hit her head on the corner of the table as she wilted to the ground. There was a sickening thump as her body hit the cheap orange shag carpet covering the floor. Her hand made a feeble attempt to reach the bump that would soon form on the back of her head but it went limp.

"You took something that I wanted. This is my territory. Not yours. Not anyone else's either." Tracy's accoster tried to justify what they'd done.

"Mine, not yours." Dark eyes spied the couch. There was a pillow. It would be over soon. People needed to be warned, to be taught a lesson. As the pillow was laid over Tracy's face, a smile lit up her killer's face. *One enemy down.*

Chapter One

Valentina

Valentina Caponelli cranked the radio up and sang a little louder. The headache she'd had earlier disappeared the minute she crossed the border into Wisconsin. Big city living had its advantages, but she'd missed the small town of Lake Genoa, or as the locals just called it, Genoa. She'd done what her father wished. Her law school diploma was proudly framed and sitting in a box in the backseat of the car.

When you were born into a mafia family, you did what they expected you to do, whether you wanted to or not. Valentina excelled in school and therefore she was the one chosen to attend law school. It never hurt to have someone in the family who knew the ins and outs of the legal system, as well as what a person could and couldn't get away with. When you did something you shouldn't, they knew how to keep you from going to jail.

The only problem was that her father didn't want

her to have other any other clients outside the family. That wouldn't keep her very busy, and that was something she enjoyed doing—keeping busy. The more irons in the fire, the more Valentina excelled. The more she felt like her life had purpose and she wasn't just the spoiled mafia princess everyone expected her to be. If law was her passion, that was yet to be discovered, but she was giving it a try.

Her father also had the nerve to point out that she was getting a little long in the tooth and needed to find a man soon. Make that a nice Italian boy approved by him to marry. *Give me a break.* When did being in your mid-twenties make you an old maid? Screw the old ways. If she could be a female lawyer, why did she have to marry? Who had time to date anyway when you were studying twenty-four seven?

She tapped her fingers on the steering wheel and hummed along with the latest Carrie Underwood song. No one would ever suspect her of being a country fan with her high heels, business suits, and her hair often in a chignon. People needed to see her as a professional, and wearing her thick dark hair long while sporting blue jeans and cowboy boots just didn't cut it.

All the cramming in law school had taken its toll on her eyes. Now sporting reading glasses on occasion, her serious look had become more matronly librarian than anything else. That wasn't going to turn the heads of too many men.

It was her father who had started her morning migraine and her sudden exodus from Chicago. If her older brother, Roman, could run parts of their father's dealings from Genoa, so could she. Valentina had been away from her business, Firenza, for way too long and it was time to get back to doing something she enjoyed. Sure, law was easy and intriguing to her, but making that a success would be a huge undertaking.

Firenza was an old lakeside mansion Roman bought for her to run as a restaurant in the summertime and event center year-round. While in Chicago, they'd hired a manager to oversee the place and her sister-in-law, Madison, also helped in her absence. It didn't take her long to realize that she wanted to put her lawyer shingle out in Genoa to be close to Firenza. Heck, it was almost time for Firenza to host the Snowflake Ball again.

Roman had met his wife at last year's ball. Valentina sang along to the next tune thinking about her sibling and his lovely wife. It was hard to say which one she loved more. Madison may have been new to the family but she already felt like her sister. It had killed Valentina that she had to concentrate on the bar exam when she would've rather been more involved with the planning of their wedding.

Actually, there hadn't been too much to plan, it happened so fast. Still, it had been far too long since she'd gotten to spend time with either of them. Then again, maybe she didn't want to. They were so much in love the two could barely keep their hands off each other. All she needed was a constant reminder that there was no man in her life, no one man enough to be in her life. What self-respecting, law-abiding man would date the daughter of

Chicago's biggest crime boss anyway?

A big yawn escaped her lips. It had been a long day. Her morning discussion with her father and a late lunch with a friend had put her way behind on packing. And then there was the rush hour traffic. She wouldn't miss that or the toll roads. Wouldn't it be nice if she could ride a bike to work on the path that surrounded Lake Genoa? That brought out a giggle. She'd not ridden a bicycle in years. Could she do it in heels? Did many men in Genoa ride bikes, or were boats more their speed? Her brother was friends with one of the local motorcycle clubs, but even he would be enraged if she took up with a biker. Picturing herself as some biker dude's old lady just didn't fit. Even though they might be the only ones brave enough to take on her father. Tattoos weren't her style either.

Valentina felt hopeless. On one hand, she didn't *need* a man in her life, but on the other, it was all she thought about. What would it be like to have someone to share her hopes and dreams with? Take vacations with or just stay home and watch football on the couch together? Finding a man to love her seemed almost as impossible as winning the lottery.

Maybe she could change her name to Valentina Johnson. As if that would work. As soon as she brought the guy home to meet her parents, her secret would be exposed. She should have become a nun instead of a lawyer. Besides, no one would be able to meet her high standards anyway—he had to be perfect in her eyes. Placing her elbow on the armrest, she set her chin on her fist. Well, there was one man who fit the bill.

Officer Ryan Donavan. Just the mention of his name made her knees weak and her feet wobble in their stilettos. Even as a kid she had a crush on him. They'd gone to the same high school in Chicago. Roman and he even played football together. The man probably still pictured her as the gangly, acne-faced teenager. Valentina took after her brother, tall and lean. That probably just added to the list of undesirable traits she had that men didn't want in a woman. She was too smart, too skinny, and way too mafia.

The October day had been cloudy so the darkness of evening came fast. As her car crossed the county line it was time to turn the lights on. At least it wasn't rut season yet so there was no need to worry about randy bucks running across the road. Well, it could still happen, but it wasn't as likely. Clicking between the bright and dimmer lights, there didn't seem to be much difference. She'd have Arlo take a look when she got to her brother's place. Arlo, Roman's bodyguard slash driver slash Jack of all trades was pretty handy with cars. It was probably just a bulb out but one that would need to be fixed before she got a ticket or worse.

A favorite song came on, the one with Miranda and Carrie singing that something bad was about to happen. With a sharpie in her hand as a pretend mic, she joined in the chorus. Her head bobbed with the beat and a few bobby pins went flying. *Oh shit.* Her eyes caught the reflection of a police car parked along the side of the road. In case she'd been speeding, she let her foot off the gas but didn't hit the brake. No need to draw attention to herself by flashing her taillights. Tossing the marker to the side, Valentina took a deep breath and kept driving.

She let out a sigh of relief that he didn't follow. *So far so good.* Unfortunately, a mile down the road, bright lights flashed behind her. Cursing in two languages, she pulled over and parked. Despite the dusk, Valentina could tell that it was him in the rearview mirror, Ryan Donavan, the object of her teenage, and adult, dreams. It was hard not to admire the tall figure as he got out the car. The badge on his chest glimmered with the flashes of light from the emergency lightbar on the top of his squad car. His flashlight blinded her as he quickly glanced in the backseat of her car before settling it on her face.

"Well, if it isn't Valentina Caponelli." He holstered his flashlight and leaned a forearm on the roof of her car. "You're going a little fast, darling." He'd never called her darling before, but who was she to argue with the law.

"I didn't think I was." She batted her eyes and stuck her chest out. Hey, it worked in the movies. Officer Ryan, as she recalled, was addressed by everyone in Genoa by his first name and not the last. He took the bait and dropped his gaze to her breasts.

His eyes were a deep blue and his dark hair was ruffled by the night air. Despite the cool breeze, he wore a short-sleeve shirt that showed off his muscles to perfection. She inhaled a combination of some evergreen inspired fragrance as well as coffee and leather.

"Get out of the car." He stepped back. She didn't

move. "Now." His tone screamed he wasn't messing around and that no was not an option.

You would think that being from a family that didn't respect the law, she'd dismiss him without a second thought, but the fact was, it turned her on.

"Whatever you say, Ryan." Valentina twisted in the seat and noticed that he glanced at her legs as she swiveled and stepped out of the vehicle.

"It's Officer Donavan to you." Obviously, she wasn't among those allowed to use his given name. She rose and smoothed the winkles from her skirt.

The man just stood there. His hands were on his hips and his gaze raked her from head to toe. "Have you been drinking, Valentina?" It was okay for him to use her first name but she couldn't use his? Her lips pouted.

"Well, have you?" he repeated in a low voice that caused her heart to race.

"What?" She shook her head. "Hell no. Don't you know it's against the law to drink and drive?" She waved her fingers at him before entwining her fingers behind her back and propping against her car.

"Keep your hands where I can see them." He took a step closer and the same intoxicating cologne she first noticed when he leaned against her car entered her brain again.

She took a deep breath and narrowed her eyes. "Where would you like me to put them?" she purred. Since when had she become such a vixen? Valentina had always been a bumbling idiot whenever Ryan was around and barely able to remember her name. Now she was practically begging to be put in handcuffs. The man was so close she could feel his breath on her skin.

"Walk," he whispered in her ear.

"What?" Valentina pushed away from the car and Ryan stepped back.

"I said walk." He took out his light again and motioned to the center line. "I can't smell it but something tells me you've been hitting the bottle. You're usually a shy thing."

It was now or never if she was going to get Ryan to think of her as anything other than Roman's nerdy little sister. Strutting as sexily as she could, Valentina maneuvered the yellow stripe perfectly. When she reached the end, she did a turn that would make any runway model envious. Somewhere along the way her awkwardness had turned to grace and her timidness to confidence. "So, how did I do?"

His face hadn't changed. What was the man thinking? How she wished it was sunny out so he'd be wearing a pair of those hot mirrored sunglasses, but then she wouldn't be able to read his eyes then either.

"You shouldn't be driving in those shoes."

She turned her foot at an angle. "You don't like my shoes? They cost me a thousand dollars."

"I don't care what they cost. They're dangerous. Your foot could slip off the pedal and cause an accident."

Her heart sank. All he was interested in was public safety, and he'd probably say the same thing to every chick in a pair of pumps.

"Maybe I like living dangerously," she tossed out while sauntering back to her car.

Ryan grabbed her arm and pulled her tightly to his chest. "Is that so?"

Finally, she was where she yearned to be for so long. "Yes, but only if you're there to protect and serve me." It was corny but it brought a smile to his lips.

"I can definitely do that." His mouth lowered to hers.

The song ended and the DJ gave the weather report for tomorrow, mild and partly cloudy.

Valentina shook off the fantasy that had floated through her mind for the last few minutes. To heck with shoes being dangerous, driving while thinking about Ryan Donavon could be deadly. Just thinking about a kiss had her eyes closing for a brief moment.

It was all a dream. The man didn't know she existed, wouldn't be interested in her if he did, and a man in law enforcement would never end up with mafia royalty. End of story. She rubbed her eyes and yawned again.

Out of nowhere a huge buck hopped onto the road. *Holy shit!* It happened in a flash. Her foot hit the brake. She jerked the steering wheel. The deer stopped but not fast enough to avoid hitting the side of her car. Her car skidded out of control and off the road. The front hit a tree and came to a stop.

"Oh my god, oh my god, oh my god." Her hands shook like the leaves on the oak she just hit. A few of them dropped down and landed on her cracked hood. The car looked totaled but at least she was alive.

Chapter Two

Ryan

Officer Ryan Donavan took a sip of his gas station coffee. After wrinkling up his nose, he dumped the rest of it out the car window. It was best not to drink caffeine this late in the night anyway. Insomnia kept him up most evenings. The java would just aggravate the situation even more.

It was a quiet evening, as were most nights. Lake Genoa was a peaceful place to live. The moon above wasn't full, it was Monday, and the Packers had a game so there was no reason for any traffic to be on the road until the game ended. Then he'd have to keep an eye out for anyone driving under the influence. If there was one thing he hated, it was drunk drivers. The need to get out of town was strong so he picked a side road to park, listen to the game on the radio, and get a few minutes of peace.

He preferred to eat alone. There was nothing worse than sitting down at a diner to eat and then be pulled away on a call before he could even lift his fork. Then there were those who just wanted to talk and talk. They often wanted to complain that he should be out chasing criminals and not taking time for a break. Everyone had to eat, even cops. Especially if they were working a twelve-hour shift or longer.

The gas station sandwich wasn't much better than the coffee. Placing the sandwich back in the wrapper, he settled for the bag of chips instead. It would be very dark soon and then he'd have to get back to town and see if anything was going on at the station. The radio had been silent for an hour, just the other patrolmen checking in and signing off. It was fall so there were even less people working. In the summertime, the force hired an extra eight to ten part-time patrol officers, but the tourist season was over so things had really slowed down. It was a nice break.

A set of headlights hauling ass down the road caught his attention and he halted the chip halfway to his mouth. Ryan grabbed the radar gun and pointed it at the oncoming car. The gun read fifty-eight. Not fast enough to ruin someone's evening. The driver was probably in a hurry to get home and watch the game; that's where he'd be if he had a choice. It'd be great to be home with his feet up on the coffee table, a can of beer in one hand, and, if he was lucky, a girl on the couch next to him. *Good luck with that.* Ryan set the gun to the side and bit into his chip. He couldn't remember the last time he'd been on a date. He worked too much, dated too little, and that left him with the disposition of an angry bear.

With much prodding from his patrol buddies, he'd asked out the new girl in town, Arianne, a waitress at the Waffle House. She was a known badge bunny. The kind who got their kicks from dating, if you could call a one-night stand dating, cops. He wasn't looking for that kind of relationship but he'd caved and asked her to a dance at the town's western bar, The Dew Drop Inn. As he'd waited for his midnight plate of waffles, he reluctantly agreed to take her there Friday night as there was a big name singer in town. With any luck, the evening would end with her in his bed, but for some reason it just wasn't as appealing as it should be.

A flashy red sports car flew by, causing him to bite his tongue when he recognized the vehicle. Valentina Caponelli. What he wouldn't give to have her naked and pressed up against him. The car was a perfect match for the bright red lipstick she usually wore and the soles of those fancy dancy shoes she pranced around in. If there was a list of women out of his league, that mafia princess would be at the top. Yet, he couldn't help thinking about her anytime he got a spare moment. He'd run into her sister-in-law not too long ago and found out she was a lawyer now.

Valentina had been a few years younger than him in school, but even then she was very smart and very snobby. The girl would never even look at him and ran whenever he was near. Still, a man yearned for what he wanted whether it was a good choice or not. Maybe that was why he didn't date much—every woman paled in comparison to her. A man could dream though. He finished the chips, crumpled up the bag, and tossed it on the passenger seat. He'd clean up the mess at the end of the shift.

Turning up the volume of the game, he hoped to clear the vision of her beautiful face. It didn't work. In his eyes, she was the most beautiful woman in the world. The fact that she was super smart and driven to succeed just increased his admiration. Ryan yawned and stretched.

"Donavan?" the dispatcher called out his name.

"Here," he responded on the radio pinned near his shoulder.

"We have a deer versus car out your way. Can you handle it?"

"Sure." He started the engine. "Any injuries that you know of?"

"Not sure, but the woman said she didn't need an ambulance."

"Okay, give me the location." It was right over the hill from him, less than two miles to be exact. Holy shit, could it be Valentina? Unless someone had come from the north, that was the only car he'd seen go by lately. Ryan put the car in gear, hit the siren, and turned onto the road.

"I'm on my way," he radioed.

It was less than a minute before he could see that his worst fear was true. Valentina's car sat by the side of the road, the hazard lights blinking. The driver's door was wide open and a pair of shapely legs stuck out, a shoe dangled off one foot and the other sat on the road.

Shit. He flew out of his car as fast as he could and rushed to the car. "Val? Val?" Her body lay face down and her head was near the floor of the passenger seat. Was she dead? His throat tightened and he leaned over to touch the side of her throat for a pulse just as she reared up and knocked skulls with his. He jerked up and his hat flew off, landing on the ground with an empty thud.

The woman he feared might be dead sprang at him like a wild cat. "Don't touch me," she screamed. Her eyes were wide and blood dripped from her nose.

Ryan raised his hands in surrender. Maybe she was in shock. "It's me, Valentina. Ryan, Ryan Donavan."

Her shoulders dropped and she leaned back against the seat. "Am I ever happy to see you."

"Well, you weren't a second ago. I thought I was going to have to tase you." He hoped the jab would set her at ease, but what worked on most people didn't mean it would work on Valentina.

She carefully got out of the car and took a step. Valentina wobbled. One limb was at least four inches shorter than the other. He bent to grab her lost shoe and set it next to her bare foot. Valentina slipped it on and was on level footing again.

"What were you doing anyway? Are you all right?" He tried to get a good look at her eyes to see if she was having trouble focusing or for any sign of a head injury.

"I hit a deer. A huge deer. It came out of nowhere." She waved her hands in the air to show that the animal was at least ten feet high. "I was getting out of the car and realized my nose was bleeding. I thought I had some tissue under the seat." Her hand went to her nose and was covered with more fresh blood. "Oh no." Valentina paled and Ryan guided her back to the driver's seat.

"I'll be right back. I have a first aid kit in the car." He grabbed his hat on the way and placed it back on his head.

Ryan hurried back. A pair of latex gloves on his hands as he draped a blanket across her shoulders and gently touched some tissue to her nose to stop the bleeding. It didn't appear broken.

"Did you hit your head on the steering wheel?"

She shook her head and the fresh scent of her shampoo flirted with his nose.

"What happened that your nose is bleeding?" After much prodding, Valentina finally admitted that as she got out of the car to check the damage, her ankle turned and she hit her nose on the door. The woman may have been hot, but she was obviously not very coordinated. "It also has been known to happen when I am under stress."

The radio attached to his shoulder broke the silence and the dispatcher asked for the status of his situation.

Valentina spoke up before he could answer. "I'm fine and I don't need a wrecker. I can just call Arlo."

Ryan pressed the button on his radio. "Everything is under control. No further assistance needed."

Ryan handed her an ice pack to hold over her nose as he rose and checked out the damage to her car. It would need to be towed. The passenger side front end was toast. It was probably even totaled. A small sports car was no match for a buck, even a small one. Using his flashlight, he searched the ditch but saw no deer. Hopefully, the animal escaped with only a few bruises.

When he returned to Valentina's side, her hands shook as she struggled to push the right buttons on her phone. She was eventually successful and he heard someone answer on the other end of the line. He recognized the voice of her brother, Roman.

Taking the phone from her hands, Ryan said, "Roman, this is Officer Ryan. Valentina is fine but her car is out of commission." He paused as her brother asked the usual questions. "Looks like a deer ran out, she hit him on the side, and then slid in the ditch and hit a tree. She's a little shaken up but I can take her to the hospital and get her checked out."

That brought out a long string of Italian and grabbing for the phone by his patient. After giving the cell back to Val to argue it out with her sibling, it was finally settled that Ryan would drive her to the Caponelli compound and Arlo would take care of sending a tow. He radioed back to the station where he was going and what was going on. The Caponelli family liked to keep a low profile, that was for sure.

After gathering all her belongings, which included several suitcases, a laptop, briefcase, and purse, he loaded them and her into his squad car.

"It smells in here," Valentina commented.

It figured the vehicle would be beneath her status, but he laughed anyway. "You have tissue stuck up both nostrils and can still smell?" He was used to the stench of a squad car. It was a nauseating combination of stale junk food in the front seat, and puke, sweat, and other bodily fluids from not so clean previous inhabitants in the backseat.

Ryan buckled his seatbelt and checked to make sure Val had done hers, but she just sat there crying. The hot shot lawyer, wild cat mafia princess he'd heard could stare down anyone but her father, sat there sobbing. Her shoulders jerked and silent tears streamed down her cheeks.

He'd comforted many people in very stressful situations, but suddenly, with Valentina, all that training went out the window and joined his gas station coffee on the pavement. Ryan briefly considered handing her the comfort teddy bear for kids but somehow that didn't seem right either.

"It will be okay, Val. I didn't see any blood, I'm sure the deer will be fine."

"It's not that. Not that I'm not relieved that I didn't kill Bambi, but it just added to my already messed up day."

"Want to talk about it?" He reached across to buckle her in.

"No." That was her answer, but it didn't stop her from talking and talking. It all started with a conversation with her father, a stressful morning, too much traffic, too much coffee, and ended with a run-in with wildlife. The most shocking information was that tidbit about her crime boss father. It was common knowledge that Roman had tried to cut as many ties as he could and go into legit businesses, but it shocked the hell out of him that his sister did as well.

Maybe it shouldn't have been a surprise, but Valentina had always dressed the part. She was always the submissive daddy's girl, at least that was what he remembered from school. Maybe things had changed. What hadn't changed was that whenever he caught a glimpse of her, the woman was always impeccably donned in designer clothes and shoes that probably cost more than he made in a month. As much as he always admired her from afar, right now she seemed almost within reach.

Without even thinking, and as much as the seatbelts allowed, Ryan pulled her into his arms. The tears continued to fall as he gently stroked her hair and whispered soothing words. Her dark hair had fallen from its clip and some of the curls lay along her back. It was softer than he could have ever imagined. Having her in his arms was more than he could have ever imagined. She was always the unattainable one. If her brother could see them now, Ryan was positive there would be hit called out on him in no time flat. Roman would probably have his buddy, Dominic, carve him up in little pieces and toss them into Lake Michigan. Ryan couldn't prove it but there was no doubt in his mind that the two were behind the deaths of not one but a few missing people. Obviously, going legit didn't include not killing people. Sure, those misfortunate souls were bad to the bone and the town was better off without them, but it still didn't sit well. Laws were meant to be followed.

There was no resisting the urge to pull her closer. The fact that she didn't seem to mind was heaven on earth. The moment was cut short by the buzzing of her cell phone. Sniffling, she twisted out of his embrace and answered the call.

"Yes?"

He heard the unmistakable voice of her brother asking where she was.

"We are on our way. Don't worry. I'm in good hands."

Ryan couldn't help but notice the pink blush to her cheeks before he started the car. If he didn't get her to Roman's soon, there would be a convoy of black SUVs here any minute to retrieve her. Her brother continued his inquisition.

"Yes, yes, we are on our way." She ended the call with a growl. "Sometimes he drives me just as crazy as my father."

"You are lucky to have so many who care for you. Never forget that." He'd lost both parents at an early age and had no siblings. Ryan made a U-turn on the road then turned off the lightbar on the roof. There was no hurry, and the thought of her leaving his car so soon left a sense of loneliness he hadn't felt in a long time.

"I am. It just gets a little suffocating sometimes."

He remained silent as they drove the short distance to town.

"I'm sorry, Ryan," Valentina said after a few minutes. "About your parents, I mean. I know you think that—" He took his hand off the wheel and she paused.

"Don't. It happened a long time ago."

"But…" she tried again before stopping. It really needed to be said, but he obviously didn't want to

23

hear it.

It was a quiet ride to Roman's house.

Chapter Three

Valentina

Valentina slammed the squad car door harder than she intended. Her brother came out the front door, followed closely by Madison.

"Are you all right?"

"I'm fine."

They spoke at the same time and Madison enclosed her in a hug. It was hard to admit but she needed that embrace more than she could imagine.

"I'm just a little shaken up." Valentina took a step back and gave a nod to Officer Ryan, who now stood by the front of the car. He looked so handsome in his uniform. The tie and hat were more formal than the fantasy she'd had of him but he was none the less for it. "I'm very thankful Ryan was there so quickly. I'm probably overreacting but it scared me."

Her brother stepped over to the officer and held out his hand. "Thanks, Ry. Appreciate you coming to the aid of my sister."

"Just doing my job." They shook hands. A few crickets sounded and you could hear the soft waves of the water off the lake. "Well, I'd better get back. Take care, Val. Madison." He nodded to both of them, got in his car, and drove off.

"That was odd," Madison said. "We should have invited him in."

"He's on duty, dear." Roman kissed her on the cheek. "But I love how thoughtful you are."

Valentina resisted the urge to roll her eyes. She loved Madison like a sister but sometimes they were too much. Way too much for someone with no love life. Her eyes focused on the taillights as they headed down the driveway. He appeared to hit the brake lights once and she could have sworn their gazes locked in the rearview mirror, but that would have been too much to hope for. It was clear that Ryan Donavan wanted nothing to do with her and her family. It was foolish to think there could ever be anything between the two with her family history. She couldn't blame him. They were from two different worlds.

"Val?" Roman called from the front of the house, holding the door open for her. "Are you coming in?"

"Oh, yes. Sorry." Her heels clicked on the cement sidewalk and up the stairs. "I guess I'm still a little shaken up." If her brother knew about the daydream she'd had about Ryan just minutes before the crash, he'd be shaking her by the shoulders, trying to knock some sense into her.

Warmth surrounded her as soon as she stepped inside. Since Madison had moved in, Roman's house had become more of a home. The mansion had always been impeccably decorated but now it had a lived in aspect that wasn't there before.

The roaring fireplace drew her closer and she held her hands out to the flames. What did Ryan's home look like? Dammit, there she was thinking about the handsome patrolman again. Was it possible she'd hit her head, because she seriously had Ryan on the brain.

"Here, I made you a hot toddy." Madison held a mug out and Valentina eagerly wrapped her fingers around the warm ceramic. It smelled wonderful.

"What is it?" She took a sip. The heat and alcohol warmed her from cheeks to toes.

"It's a new bourbon we're trying out. Do you like it? Oh, and it has some lemon and honey in there too." One of the new ventures Roman was involved in to make the family business more legit was a winery.

"I know you're making wine, but bourbon too?"

"It never hurts to branch off in other areas." Madison beamed as her husband wrapped an arm around her waist from behind.

Valentina took another drink to take her mind off the love birds. It did the trick, but soon Ryan's smile flashed again in her mind.

"You must really like it." Her sister-in-law's eyes sparkled.

"Huh?"

"You have this dreamy look on your face." Nothing seemed to get past Madison, and as Valentina sneaked a peek at her brother, it was obvious he noticed her reaction as well.

Roman's phone sounded and he walked off to take the call.

"Are you sure you're okay, Val?" Madison titled her head, worry lines crossing her forehead.

"Yes, yes. I'm just distracted. That's probably one of the reasons I didn't see that deer." She exhaled loudly and scrunched up her nose. "Things didn't go very well with my father today."

"They never do with Roman and him either." Madison motioned to her husband before embracing Val and whispering in her ear. "Tomorrow, you and me. We're going to the spa."

"That sounds heavenly," she whispered back. A massage would be wonderful. Her muscles ached from being so uptight. Although she could also think of another, more pleasurable way to unwind, but that would involve a certain cop who seemed to want nothing to do with her. "It's a date."

"Great." Madison glanced down at Val's now empty glass. "Would you like another?"

"Ah, no. Another one and I'll need help getting up the stairs." She eased herself down into the nearest chair. "Oh no. I left my bags in the squad car."

"It's all taken care of," Roman announced as he came back in the room. "Donavan realized he still had them. He came back and flagged one of the guards down in the driveway. Should be here any minute."

"Ryan?" Her heart fluttered.

"No, your bags." Her brother stepped in front of her and narrowed his eyes. "Madison, would you mind if I had a word with my sister alone?"

"Not at all." She kissed his cheek. "I was about to turn in anyway. I'll see you upstairs. Night, Val. See you in the morning."

Valentina nodded and then crossed her arms in front of her chest. Roman wanting to speak to her alone was never a good thing.

"Yes?" She crossed her legs and cocked her head.

"Don't *yes* me. What the hell happened?"

"What do you mean what happened? I hit a damn deer."

"That's not what I'm talking about. You were supposed to stay in Chicago." He stared down at her, his hands on his hips.

"So you've spoken to Father?"

"Yes, he wanted you to stay and work for the family."

Valentina rose to her feet. "I can work for the family here. But that is the extent of my family obligation. I will not accept any personal arrangements, if you know what I mean."

It was slight but Roman winced. Roman had been promised to marry the daughter of one of the other families. It was either that or be killed. Who would have ever in a million years thought that at the last minute the impending bride would end up being the one he really loved. Valentina, on the other hand, would not be so lucky. Ryan was on the right side of the law and he was Irish. There was no way her father would ever see him as anything but.

"You don't have to remind me of what almost happened to me. You can stay here as long as you want."

Val's shoulders relaxed and she smiled. "Thanks, but I plan on getting a place of my own and starting my own law office."

"What about your obligations to Firenza?"

"That's another reason I had to leave. It's going to take a while to build up a clientele so I'm only going to be at the law office a few days a week. That will leave plenty of time to keep up with things at Firenza."

"Good. I'll have Arlo find you a place to stay."

"No." She stomped her foot. It was childish but she was tired and cranky.

"No?" He lifted one eyebrow.

"No. Thanks for the help, but I need to start doing things on my own. I told Father I wanted my independence and I wouldn't be very self-sufficient if I relied on you to do everything for me."

Roman groaned and wandered over to stand by the fire. "Fair enough."

Valentina gave her brother a quick hug and, after spying Arlo entering the front door with her bags, headed his way. Roman reached out, grabbed her wrist, and stopped her in her tracks.

"One more thing."

"What?" The grip on her arm tightened.

"Keep your distance from Donavan."

"What? Why?" She tried to shake off his hand but he held tight. "It's a small town. We're bound to bump into each other."

"It's dangerous," Roman warned.

"Dangerous? He's a cop. I would think I would be safer around him than anyone." She avoided meeting his eyes. "Not that I would be around him or anything."

"You are interested. I've caught you staring at him many times. Hell, I even saw on your Facebook page that you were following the Lake Genoa Police Department page."

"I'm a lawyer. It's important for me to stay on top of all things legal and what's happening in the community."

"Don't lie to me." A lesser man would be shaking in his shoes, but Val was his sister and knew he would never hurt her. Twisting out of his grip in a move Roman had taught her, Val turned and pointed her finger in his face.

"I'm not lying. You want the truth?"

"Yes." He waved a confused-looking Arlo back out the door he came in.

"Am I intrigued with the man? Yes. Do I think he is handsome? Hell yes. Do I think he would ever date someone like me?" She frowned. "No."

"And why the hell not?" Roman grumbled as he walked to the bar and poured himself one of those wicked strong bourbons.

"You know why."

"No, I don't. Any man would be proud to have you in his life. I just don't want it to be him."

"Well, I don't think you have anything to worry about, then." She picked up her purse and headed over to her bags. "It's obvious that he isn't interested in me."

"Obviously, he's smart but has piss pour taste in women."

Her brother was trying to make her feel better despite the fact that he wanted her to have nothing to do with Ryan.

"Well, you and I both know the main reason he would die before having a relationship with me."

Roman turned to face her. "Oh, yeah? And what is that?"

"Because our father would probably kill him if he ever touched me."

Chapter Four

Ryan

Ryan's hopes for a quiet rest of the evening were dashed as soon as the next call came in—an unknown disturbance in the town's only trailer park. Lake Genoa was a tourist town in the southeastern part of Wisconsin. In the summer, the place was practically bursting with travelers from the windy city of Chicago. Very few of those visitors would ever dream of stepping foot in this poor neighborhood. It may have been called Lake Shore Park, but there was no water in sight.

He hit the siren and the car's red and blue lights reflected off the windows of the houses he passed as he sped toward that part of town. Apparently, another squad was already on scene but they were not giving much info over the radio. That was not a good sign.

It didn't take long for him to get to Lake Shore Park. Already, a few of the residents were outside their homes, some in bathrobes and others in coats or orange hunting jackets. Tyler, a young man Ryan had dealt with before, could be seen in the shadows. The light from his phone lit up his face. He was probably hoping to catch something he could send to the local news. The youngster hated cops. Hell, if the brat would keep his nose clean, they'd never have to see each other again.

After notifying dispatch that he'd reached the scene, Ryan got out of the car.

"Better watch your step, pig. I got you on video," Tyler taunted.

He flashed him a big, fake smile and kept walking. Who had time for this shit? A screen door squeaked. Ryan slowed when he spied Nathan, one of his fellow patrolmen, step out the front door of the trailer. Even in the dim light he could see his face was pale.

"Nate. What've we got?" Ryan said in a hushed tone.

Nate narrowed his eyes at Ty.

Ryan turned and pointed his finger at the boy with the phone. "You. Go home. Now."

Ty gave him a middle finger and stomped off.

Taking a deep breath, Ryan returned his attention back to Nate. "What's up?"

"It's Tracy Martin."

The name was familiar but he couldn't place a face.

"The new cashier at the dairy mart."

He finally pictured the petite blonde clearly. "This her home?" He nodded his head toward the trailer.

"Yeah. The owners called when she didn't show.

34

Had the weekend off but was supposed to be in today. Said she never misses work." Nate scratched his forehead. "Door was locked so we looked in the window and noticed her lying on the floor. We broke the door down." His voice cracked. "Tracy was on the floor. Dead." Nathan shook his head. "She's my age. I just don't understand it."

"What the hell?" Ryan's fatigue vanished. Finding someone dead was, thankfully, an uncommon thing in this small town, usually only happening with the elderly. Tracy had to be twenty-five or twenty-six. What could have caused her death?

"What happened? Any sign of a struggle or foul play?"

"Your guess is as good as mine. Looks like she fell and hit her head. I don't think she was involved with anyone. At least her boss didn't think so when I asked if they'd checked all the places she might be." He cursed and glanced down at his feet. "I guess I should tell you this."

"What is it?" The night was getting stranger by the minute.

"We went out a couple times." Nathan looked him in the eye. "Nothing too serious but we did have a good time together. I just can't believe she is gone."

"I'm sorry." It was clear that her death had affected him. "Anything else you need to tell me before I go in?"

"No, but it's not pretty." The pitch of his voice got higher with each word.

"Death scenes never are." Ryan placed a hand on

the other man's shoulder. "Well, I better take a look."

"I've called the coroner and the funeral home." Nate followed on his heels.

"Has anyone else been in the place since you got here?"

"Just the super, Danny, and me. She's in there taking some photos."

"Good." Ryan took one last glance at the faces of those around the neighborhood before stepping into Tracy's home. They were just staring, looks of confusion and concern on their faces.

The trailer was small but clean. Everything seemed normal, except for the dead body in the middle of the floor. The ugly carpet was short and now featured a small blood stain beneath the head of the victim.

Danny, short for Danielle, was the only female member of the Genoa police force. The lightness of her skin reflected the light from the overhead ceiling fan. So intent on her job, she jumped when the door slammed behind Ryan and Nate. The blue latex gloves she sported were a stark contrast to the black camera in her hand.

The dead woman lay on her back on the floor. Dark streams of mascara ran down her otherwise perfectly painted face. She appeared to be wearing leggings, a fuzzy sweater, and some high heels. Had she planned on going out for the night? A basket of laundry sat nearby, as well as some boxes. It appeared as if she fell and hit her head, but there was nothing lying on the floor in that area that would cause someone to trip.

"Damn," Ryan cursed, and his fellow officer raised her eyes to meet his.

"Damn is right. This is some fucked up shit." Danielle may have looked like a *Playboy* center fold dressed in a uniform, but she had more street smarts than anyone on the force. She also swore like a sailor. "Looks like trauma to the head—the corner of the table appears to be the impact object."

"Do you think it was accidental or intentional?" The blueish color of the skin along the back of her neck suggested that she had died in that position.

"Hard to tell at this point." She snapped some more photos. "But there's a pillow lying on the floor next to the body. I also found something."

Danny pointed to the book on the counter. "It's here. In the appointment book. I guess she was old school and wrote everything down instead of keeping it on her phone." She tapped a gloved finger on the cover. "She had a date with someone by the name of A. Man at nine on Friday night."

"Did you find anyone or any places with A in their names in the book or on her phone?"

"I will take them with me and do a search. I have to get back to the station soon."

"Good job." His heart ached for the woman on the floor. A life cut short was never easy to see. He dreaded contacting her family to give them the horrible news. "Get me the next of kin as well."

"Don't worry. Nate and I can do that."

"Thanks. I'll stay here, then." The woman would not be left alone. She deserved to have someone with her. "Nate, how long before the coroner will be here?"

He hoped Nathan wouldn't vomit. The guy looked green around the gills and was inching toward the door. It was hard enough being around dead bodies, let alone someone you knew. A sickening smell had settled in the tiny room, making it difficult for all of them to take deep breaths. Tracy had been like this for a few days as least.

"Dr. Bob's already on the way, should be here any minute now. At least that was what the answering service said."

In their county, anyone could be elected coroner despite having no medical experience. They just had to show up at the scene, pronounce the person dead, and notify family members after signing the death certificate. At least the current holder of the title had some medical experience, even if it was more of the animal variety. Dr. Robert Hutter was the large animal veterinarian at the Hoof and Paws vet clinic, but everyone just called him Dr. Bob. The county's last coroner was a used car salesman who drank himself to death.

"Do you think it could be a homicide?" Danny stood up. "I have an odd feeling about this."

"I'm not ruling anything out."

He didn't know Tracy well but the dairy mart was open twenty-four hours a day. After he finished up here, he'd be stopping by to see what her coworkers had to say. Maybe some late-night customer followed her home. The door was locked from inside but she could have let someone in. A young woman didn't just fall and kill herself every day. It didn't add up.

"The funeral home is here to remove the body."

Nate popped his head outside the screen door. What a relief it would be to be outside in the cool, crisp air. The stuffiness and stench of the room was getting to him also. A few beads of sweat formed on his forehead.

"They'll have to wait until the coroner gets here. Get me an ETA from Dr. Bob's answering service now."

Ryan's cell phone buzzed. It was a text from an unknown number.

Thanks again for coming to my rescue. Val

At first it shocked him that she had his number, but then he remembered giving her his card when Madison experienced a break-in at her store. The message was a welcome escape from where he stood now. Any other time, he'd call back just to hear her voice. Despite the fact they had no future, one could dream.

His gaze fell to the young woman on the floor in front of him. It was lonely in the presence of a deceased person, even if it was someone you didn't know well. Now was definitely not the time to call Valentina.

"I got ahold of the vet. He's on the way. Had to deliver a breech calf."

Living in a rural area was never boring, that was for sure. Ryan took a blanket off the couch and laid it over Tracy's body. Danny had taken enough photos—she deserved her dignity.

"Thanks, Nate."

Ryan tucked the phone back in his pocket. It was

late, he'd call Valentina tomorrow. Tracy deserved all his attention right now. He'd find out what happened if it took all night.

Valentina

Once she made up her mind, things moved fast. After a few days relaxing at her brother's house it was time to move out. Valentina patted her purse that held the newly signed lease for a small downtown office space. Despite her claim for independence, the vacant spot Madison suggested for her was just too good to pass up. She also found a place to live. It was one of those old turn-of-the-century mansions in the historic district.

She could see clients in the morning, if she had any, and head off to work at Firenza for the rest of the day. Heck, her new home was so close to both, Valentina could walk to each place. Her next stop was the local auto dealership. It wasn't well known but her family was big into car sales. Some vehicles just came with more than the usual add-ons. This time, however, she was buying from someone else. There would be no more relying on her family if she was going to make her own way in life.

After a few signatures, Valentina left her little red sports car, dents and all, in the lot and drove off in a shiny new silver four-wheel-drive pickup. If her parents and friends could see her, they would be shocked, to say the least.

Valentina parked her new vehicle in front of the tourism office where Madison worked. It was sunny but still a chilly fall day. She straightened her scarf in the visor mirror and studied her makeup. She never knew who she might run in to, but chances were it wouldn't be the handsome officer who came to her rescue Monday night. Valentina slammed the truck door harder than planned. The same handsome officer who never bothered to return her text.

"Men," Valentina said under her breath, and entered Madison's place of business.

"Hey, Val," her sister-in-law greeted. "To what do I owe this surprise?"

"Just seeing if you wanted to do lunch or something." She took a seat in a nearby chair.

"I will go for the 'or something'. I need something to wear tonight. If you give me a minute, I can close up for lunch."

"Sure."

Maddy grabbed her purse, put the out to lunch sign up, and locked the door.

"What's the occasion?" Val barely had time to warm up before she was ushered back out the door.

"It's kind of a Sadie Hawkins slash western dance. I need cowboy boots, hat, and a sexy dress."

"Is Roman going? I've got to see him decked out in jeans." Just the thought of her brother dressed as a cowboy brought on the giggles. He was always impeccably dressed, like he just stepped off the cover of *Gentlemen's Quarterly*. Did the man even own anything besides designer suits?

"The Sadie Hawkins part means he can't back out, and believe me, he will be well rewarded for

41

going along."

"TMI. TMI." She loved Roman and Madison, but sometimes they were just too much. "Where is it? Can anyone go?"

"Of course. And I heard from a reliable source that a certain knight in shining armor will be there also." Maddy wiggled her eyebrows.

"Who? Officer Ryan?" What was the use of wishing for something that would never happen? Not to mention she was still pissed at him for not returning her message.

"What? I thought I noticed some heat between the two of you."

"Well, if there was, it was all on my side." She pulled on the ends of her scarf. "I sent him a text that night to thank him and he never even bothered to respond."

"I think he's had his hands full this week. There might have been a murder." There was a frown shadowing her face. "They're still trying to figure out the cause of death, but Roman seems to think there was foul play."

"What? Here?" Bad crimes like that happened in big cities every day, but not in the quiet little town of Genoa.

"Yes. Don't you read the paper? Or watch the news?" Madison asked.

"No, I haven't had time to hook up the cable. Still, I can't see Ryan going to a cowboy dance, and he had all week to get back to me." It was insensitive to be thinking of herself. Someone died and yet her only concern was why Ryan hadn't texted her back. Her gaze dropped to the sidewalk.

"I don't think he's interested. Why would he go to something like this anyway?"

"Supposedly, he got roped into going by some of the other guys on the force." Madison unlocked her Lexus with the key fob. How Maddy knew this she didn't want to know. It wouldn't surprise her a bit if her brother had the police station bugged.

"Did you just say roped?" This was too much to resist. It might be fun after all. Valentina suddenly had the urge to go boot shopping.

Chapter Five

Ryan

Ryan nursed his beer as he surveyed the crowd. Even off duty he watched for people who didn't belong or were up to no good. So far, everything appeared normal. The only thing out of place in the bar was him. What the hell was he doing here? He'd agreed to go on a hook-up date with a badge bunny. If that didn't reek of desperation, he didn't know what did. A western bar was the last place he wanted to be on his night off. Hell, he should be out looking for Tracy Martin's killer. They still didn't have all the tests back from the autopsy but he knew in his gut a young woman like that didn't just die on her own.

He should be doing a lot of things, like returning the thank you text Valentina sent him. Ryan rubbed his chin with his hands. The whiskers were proof he hadn't had time to shave that morning. That dark-haired beauty had been on his mind ever since her accident. The scent of her perfume forever locked away in his brain. They were from two different worlds but every other woman paled next to her; everything had always dimmed next to her brightness.

"Give me a brandy." Ryan waved at the bartender. It would take something stronger than beer to wash away the feeling of Valentina in his arms. The moment had been brief when he comforted her after the accident, but the feel of her skin was burned into his for a lifetime. Why did he agree to meet Arianne tonight? The whole thing was just wrong, wrong on so many levels. Sure, there were times he went out of town to find meaningless hook-ups, he had needs just like anyone else, but this was too close to home and people talked.

The bartender slid the drink his way and Ryan downed it in one sip. Dammit, that was stupid. He needed his wits about him if it was going to break things off gently. Any more to drink and he would be kissing the limit for drunk driving and be stuck here. No sneaking out the back before Arianne spotted him.

Ryan wasn't one to stand up a woman, but chances were Arianne wouldn't miss him. She was probably with someone new right now. Her reputation for being open to anything and anyone was known all over the station. The best thing would be to just stop things before they started. Be honest and admit he wasn't interested. Cut the cord. Rip the bandage off. Damn, he was in a miserable mood.

A delicate hand touched his arm. She was here. It was now or never. He touched her hand

45

sympathetically—it was time to face the truth. There was no sense postponing things any longer. It was best to just do it quick and fast.

"Look, I'm sorry, but I'm just not interested." He swirled around on the barstool and came face to face with Valentina. The hurt on her face was as clear as the water in Lake Genoa. Val withdrew her hand and stepped back as if burned.

"Val? Wait." He jumped to his feet.

"It's okay. I just wanted to say thanks again for coming to my aid the other night." She took another step back. "I'm..." her lower lip quivered, "...sorry."

Ryan grabbed her arm. "No. No, I'm sorry. I didn't mean to say that. I thought you were someone else." He patted the stool next to him. "Please sit."

Hesitantly, she took a seat. "So, were you being hit on all night or something?"

He laughed and motioned for the bartender to get her a drink. "Something like that." After she ordered and had her drink, Ryan noticed her clothes. Instead of the usual man killer attire, Valentina was dressed more like the rest of the crowd. She was wearing very tight fitting white jeans and brown boots. From the lack of scuffs, they appeared brand new. The faded blue denim shirt on her shapely figure was open at the neck to reveal some flashy jewelry. He'd heard people call that bling, but whether hers was real or fake he had no clue. Knowing the Caponelli family, it was a good chance they were legit, and that just reinforced the fact that they were not compatible. His paycheck would never keep her in diamonds or pearls.

"So, are you going tell me about it or just stare at my chest all night?" Valentina wore a cute smirk on her face.

"I was just admiring your necklace." He motioned with the glass in his hand.

"Were you now? I never pegged you as a jewelry man." She grinned.

"I'm not. It just caught my eye."

"Madison talked me into shopping and I found this at that little boutique next to the tourism office."

He knew that place and relaxed a bit knowing it was more in his budget. Not only were there family differences, but money was an issue was well. He was by no means rich, but then his money was all earned legally. It was like there was a battle going on in his brain. One side was telling him to go for it and the other side said not to bother.

"You look nice," he added.

Her eyes widened and a smile lit up her face. "Thanks."

"You always look nice, even when you are avoiding deer on the road."

"That's sweet, and I meant it when I said I appreciated you coming to my aid."

He nodded. "I was going to check on you but things got kind of crazy this week."

"I heard there was a murder. Any idea what happened?"

"I can't share anything that isn't already in the news, but I will say we are still waiting for the results of some tests." Valentina shuddered and he calmed the urge to take her in his arms. "Just to be on the safe side, don't take any unnecessary risks. I know your family has bodyguards, so use them." If Tracy had been killed, that meant her killer was still out there.

"Does that mean you're worried about me?" She raised an eyebrow.

"I worry about everyone in this town." The frown on her face proved he was saying all the wrong things. "But I would miss seeing you the most if anything were to happen to you." The alcohol had loosened his lips and her frown turned into a smile. What was he thinking admitting that?

Valentina sat up straighter, her face flushed. Music came out of nowhere as the band that was playing that night started to tune their instruments.

"So, are you here by yourself? I don't want to intrude." She traced a red-tipped finger around the rim of her glass.

"I, uh…" How did he explain he agreed to a hook-up with someone he barely knew but had no intention of going through with it? He'd sound like a crook standing outside a bank with a mask and gun saying he didn't intend to rob it. Guilty as hell.

Valentina bit her lip.

"There you are. Been waiting long?" Arianne picked the worst possible time to step between them and engulf him in a hug. With him sitting, his head was smashed between her ample breasts. The last place he wanted to be at that moment, or any time for that matter.

"Uh, Arianne. This is not a good time." He stood and Valentina muttered a quick goodbye before disappearing into the crowd. "Son of a bitch."

"What's wrong?" His date frowned and crossed her arms over her half-revealed chest. Arianne was an attractive woman but she wasn't the one he wanted.

"I know I agreed to this date but…" Ryan was at a loss for words. The alcohol that loosened his lips just moments before didn't seem to help in this situation.

"But you're not interested?" she answered for him, and took a seat. "I knew it was too good to be true that you wanted to go out."

"I did. I just…I'm sorry." He exhaled loudly. Why did everything always have to be so difficult?

"Buy me a drink and we'll call it good."

He motioned for the bartender while he searched the room for Val.

"That the one you want? The girl you were talking to?"

"It's complicated." Ryan tossed some bills on the bar.

"Then you'd best get it figured out before someone beats you to it." Arianne nodded toward the dance floor. A knot formed in his gut when he spied Valentina dancing with another man. *Well, that happened fast.*

"I didn't expect you to take this so well." The fact that she hadn't thrown her drink in his face was a pleasant surprise.

"I'm from the South." She motioned the bartender for another beer and Ryan placed more dollars on the counter. "It's all those charm school manners that my mother drilled into me."

"Really? What part of the South?" It was an effort to keep talking but it also kept him from beating the man Val was waltzing across the dance floor with to a pulp.

"Why, bless your heart. I'm a Georgia peach." Arianne winked at the young bartender. "Hello, sweet thing." She smoothed back a blonde strand that had fallen in her face and threw the bartender another glance, promising more than just a cash tip. "My mother was the perfect Southern belle and wife." She mentioned a few more things about her upbringing but it was lost on him. Arianne moved on to her next quest and Ryan was no longer needed.

"Again, I'm sorry…" he started, but she waved him off and turned to the man in front of her again.

At least Val was smiling again as the man she danced with twirled her around. The man was a local he'd stopped for a few misdemeanors. The guy may have been a jerk at times, but he knew his way around the dance floor. Ryan hated dancing, couldn't dance a step, to tell the truth. Luckily, the song ended and the band went on break. Now, he just had to get her to talk to him.

Valentina

"Thanks for the dance." She was flattered to have the man ask her to two-step after Ryan so rudely shut her down, but now she couldn't get away fast enough.

"Well, hey, little lady, the night is still young." The grip on her hand tightened.

"Yes, but like I said, thanks. I'd better go meet my friends now." Madison was supposed to be here somewhere. She searched the crowd but Maddy was nowhere in sight.

"I'll be your friend." He pulled her closer. Her chest pressed up against his.

"Let me go." Valentina struggled to get loose.

"Not before a kiss." His breath reeked of too much beer and pretzels.

"I said no." She stomped on his foot with the heel of her new cowboy boots and he let go in a hurry.

"Why you little…" The man's face was bright red and his fists tightened.

"Hey." Ryan came out of nowhere and stood between them. "Got a problem here?"

"Nope, none at all." The guy narrowed his eyes.

"Really?" Ryan's gazed locked on his but he glanced away. "Bud, is that your truck out there with the taillight still knocked out? I thought I told you to get that fixed."

"I haven't had time to do that yet."

"Well, why don't you get home now before it gets too dark. I wouldn't want to have to change that warning ticket to a violation." It was already dark but he just wanted the jerk out of there before there was trouble.

Bud's ears were bright purple. The man teetered back and forth before finally limping off the dance floor and out the door. Val let out the deep breath she hadn't realized she was holding.

"Was he bothering you?" Ryan led her away from all the staring eyes.

"I could handle him." She pulled her arm from his. It was the first time Valentina noticed what he was wearing. The black cowboy hat on his head must have been on a chair when she sat with him earlier. His tight blue jeans and cowboy boots had her practically drooling.

Valentina still didn't see Madison, so she took a seat at a table by herself. She wasn't alone for long as Ryan sat in the chair next to her.

Ryan's gaze dropped to her footwear. "Nice move with the boots. He won't be dancing the rest of the night."

"Don't you have a date to get back to?" She crossed her arms and leaned back in her chair.

"Nope."

"But you were on a date. Shouldn't you be with her?"

"I was, but it didn't turn out well."

"Then you are having as good a night as I am." She crossed her ankles. "I was supposed to meet Madison, but so far she's a no-show. Damn newlyweds."

That comment brought a smile to Ryan's lips. A bright, breathtaking smile that despite her better judgement made her toes curl.

"I got your message." He spoke louder as someone had just started the jukebox. "Like I said, I was wondering how you were doing."

"Obviously not enough to call back.

Chapter Six

The statement was bitchy but it had hurt. Maybe Roman was right. She'd been secretly chasing after a man for far too long. A man who didn't know she wanted him and obviously didn't care. Maybe it was time to give someone else a chance. "It's okay. I know you were just doing your job." It was her mistake to assume more.

Ryan shifted in his seat and ran his fingers through his hair. "It's not that…"

"I know. It's my family. You're the law. We've known each other since we were kids, yet you've had all week to get back to me. I was just being"—what was the word she searched for…needy, desperate, overly emotional?—"thankful for your help."

"There's no need to be. I was—"

She held up her hand. "Just stop. I know you were just doing your job."

"That's not all."

She cut him off again. Her father often stated that was why she'd make such a great lawyer—she never gave anyone else a chance to talk. "I've had a bad week. It was stupid of me to come here tonight." The night had held such promise. A chance to step out of her designer shoes and into the arms of a handsome man. But that was not to be. Maybe it was never meant to be for her. She would grow old alone unless her father decided to arrange a marriage for her. Which was better? She'd take the spinster route.

Goosebumps rose on her arms and she shivered just thinking about a loveless union to some friend of her father's he thought would be a good match. Heck, when she got home, Valentina would go online and order her crazy cat lady starter kit right away.

"Are you cold?" Ryan placed his hand on her forearm. An instant flash of heat shot up her arm and she pulled away. He was probably just doing his job again, making sure she was safe. Well, it was time to grow up. She rose to her feet. It was time to stop mooning after someone she idolized in high school. The man had been on a date tonight. Valentina Caponelli was no one's sloppy seconds. Her jaw tightened. She'd spent the last few years working and studying day and night to pass her exams and did a damn fine job of it too. A man who didn't appreciate her didn't deserve her.

Her legs wobbled a bit as she stood. Apparently, the one drink she'd indulged in had affected her more than she thought. She'd always been a lightweight as far as booze was concerned.

"Let me see you home."

"See me home? No, thanks." Valentina looped

her new fringe purse over her shoulder.

"Val, what the hell is wrong with you? That guy could still be out there. I don't think it's a good idea for you to go out alone." He trailed her to the door.

"Don't worry about it."

"But I do."

Yeah, right.

"Why?" she challenged. If he said it was his job again, the man would be getting a punch in the nose.

His mouth opened but nothing came out.

"You don't get it, do you?" Her finger poked his chest. "I'm the daughter of Don Caponelli and the sister of Roman Caponelli. I think I can take care of myself." The cool evening air hit her skin as soon as she stepped outside, but she was fuming inside. Everyone always thought she was weak because she dressed like a lady. Well, just because she liked to look good didn't mean she wasn't packing a Glock in her Gucci bag.

"That's not what I'm talking about and you know it." His long legs had no trouble keeping up.

Her boots echoed on the blacktop as she stomped toward her truck.

"I shouldn't have held you," he said under his breath.

"What did you say?" That was all she needed. Now he was regretting comforting her! "Well, that's just great. Afraid Roman will find out and have your head chopped off? I always thought you were more of a man than that." His eyes got big. Now she'd pissed him off. How could the evening go from bad to worse to worst ever in just a matter of minutes?

"Valentina, I could care less what your brother thinks." Ryan took a deep breath and threw up his hands. "I just want to talk, okay? To get to know you better."

Her lips twitched and she leaned against a car, staring at the ground. "Go ahead. What do you want to know?"

"I know we went to the same school and were in different grades, but that didn't mean I never noticed you." He used his fingers to lift her chin and her eyes met his. "I've always seen you. I've always wanted to reach out to you but you've been beyond my reach."

"Until I had a car accident?"

"Yes, then I couldn't resist taking you in my arms."

Could she hope that he was interested? He took her hand in his.

"But it was a mistake on my part and I never should have let it happen. It's not professional."

What the...? "What do you mean by that?" The guy was talking in circles.

"It's like you said. We're from two different worlds. After Roman and I graduated, your family and I have never crossed paths unless we had to, and it was often for bad reasons. I can see now why you never wanted to even say hi to me in school and ran the other direction whenever you caught sight of me. I thought I was not up to your standards."

"What? I never did that and I don't think that."

"Yes, you did, and you probably do. You couldn't get out of my squad car fast enough the other night."

Well, that part was true, but it was because she was scared to death of talking to him. Heck, she took debate in school to try to help get over her shyness.

"Wait, you thought I was being a snob?"

"Yeah, but—"

"How dare you call me a snob!" Valentina moved away from his grasp. How could there be any kind of future between them when they couldn't even have a civil conversation?

"Well, you sure acted like it." He placed his hands on his hips, a pissed off expression on his face.

"Well, I was just shy."

"You? Shit, you were in debate, drama, and everything else. I hear you're a big-time lawyer now. You don't do all those things and get that far by being timid."

"A big-time lawyer? I said I was shy, not timid." She mirrored his stance and stared him in the eye. How dare he dismiss her accomplishments. "Why you…you small-town cop." She took a step closer and gritted her teeth.

"What did you call me?" Ryan narrowed their distance even more. "Now I'm just some small-town cop? What the heck is wrong with that? Does that make me beneath you or something?"

She never thought of him that way. Well, him being beneath her in a bed wouldn't be that bad.

"No." The man made her insane. She could now see why her father and brother always discouraged any kind of friendship between the two whenever there was any hint that she liked the man. He was an ass. "Look, this conversation has gotten way out of hand."

"It certainly has."

Valentina stomped off. If she'd had a second longer to think, she'd have planted a heeled boot on the foot of the second bastard she'd run into this night.

"Wait," Ryan ordered, but she kept going. Screw him, and her, for ever thinking he might be the right man for her.

He grabbed her arm. "I said wait." Ryan may have been an ass but he sure looked sexy with his temper up. She fought the urge to run her fingers along his scruffy jaw. He was smoking hot tonight.

"What makes you think you can tell me what to do?"

"Damn, you are the most infuriating woman I have ever met."

"And the snobbiest," she added.

"Wow." He took a deep breath. "Look, we obviously got off on the wrong foot."

"Obviously. And if you don't let go of my arm, I will put my heel through your foot just like I did ole Bud's back in there." He dropped his hand as if she burned him.

"I was trying to apologize and…" He paused and she turned to leave. "And I've had too many beers to stop now."

Valentina kept walking. "Stop what? Making me feel even worse than I do?"

"I never meant to do that at all." His long stride easily caught up with hers. "I just wanted to say that

58

no matter the situation, I've never taken anyone in my arms when I was working but you." She stopped. "With you, I couldn't help it."

Ryan stepped in front of her. "I always noticed you in school. I could see even then that you would become a great beauty, and you were always smart. Smart enough to not want anything to do with me. I couldn't help myself. I wanted to make you feel better and, selfishly, I wanted to feel you in my arms just once even if it was for just a brief moment."

Her mouth opened and she could see her breath in the cold. The frigid air must have frozen her brain because she swore she just heard Ryan Donavan admit to liking her. Well, wanting to hold her, but what was the other stuff about? Insecurity? Mistrust of her family?

"I just wanted to say I'm sorry." He flashed a weak smile. "I'll see you to your car."

"Wait, what?"

"I'll see you safely to your car."

"No, not that. You tell me you like me and then you just become Officer Ryan again?"

"It's obvious you don't feel the same way."

"Maybe I do feel that way, but that doesn't mean I'm just going to fall into your arms now that you said something." It was what she had hoped for but things just spun out of control and became awkward. She lifted and dropped her shoulder. "A girl likes to be wooed and, you know, go on dates and—"

Her next words were cut off when his mouth touched hers. It happened so fast and then it was over. The kiss was brief yet brilliant. She licked her lips. Her heart raced.

"Let's try that again." Ryan tucked a piece of hair behind her ear and pressed her up against someone's truck. Even through her clothes her backside chilled against the cold metal. Her mouth opened slightly as his lips touched her again. This time it was slow and sweet, long and luscious. His kiss was laced with the heady taste of brandy. Never a fan of brandy, it was now something she was eager to acquire a taste for.

Never did she image her evening would end in a kiss from Ryan Donavan. Sure, she'd thought of it many times, but thinking and doing were totally different. The intoxicating assault on her mouth increased and then it was gone.

Opening her eyes, she stared into dark blue ones.

"Are you wooed yet?" He winked.

The nerve of the man! "Are you so arrogant that you think one kiss will have me at your feet?" Valentina slipped out of his arms and the lack of warmth chilled her to the bone.

"Having you at my feet isn't exactly where I picture you." He had a smirky smile on his face.

"Oh yeah, and where is that?" She rubbed her arms and shuffled from foot to foot.

"Let's just say I would have to do a helluva lot more wooing for that to happen."

A gasp escaped her lips. After waiting so long for the man she yearned for to notice her, he had her head spinning, but it wasn't time yet to forgive him for calling her snobby. That hurt. She scowled and headed to her truck.

"What the hell, Val? I tell you that I've always had a thing for you, kiss your socks off, and now you leave in a huff. Maybe you're not just a snob but a tease as well."

She halted and turned slowly around. Her fists were tight and her jaw set. His face was unreadable. Was he joking? Was he seeing how she would respond? "How dare you say that, and as you can obviously see, my socks are still on."

Ryan laughed loudly. "I do dare." He stepped closer and she breathed in the cool air mixed with his aftershave. It was a refreshing scent of soap and pine. "You aren't going to make this easy on me, are you?"

"You don't look like a man who likes things easy," she challenged.

"It's like I said, you are a very smart woman, Valentina. I do like a challenge and mysteries. That's one of the reasons I became a cop. I like figuring out who the bad guys, and girls, are."

"And you think I'm a bad girl?"

His face sobered. "Your family is."

"I am not my family." It was so frustrating never to be judged for the person she was but who her father was.

"The hell you aren't." The voice came from behind her. Valentina spun around and came face to face with her brother.

Chapter Seven

"What the hell is going on here?" Roman directed the question at Val before turning to Ryan. "Ry, are you fucking bothering my sister?" He held up a gloved fist.

"Roman, please." Val stepped between the two men.

"No, we're just working a few things out." Ryan put his hands in his pockets.

Roman ignored him and kissed his sister's forehead. "Sorry we're late."

"Roman refused to wear what I picked out," Madison explained.

"I don't do cowboy attire," he mumbled. The man was decked out in his usual designer suit.

"Well, you're here, that's all that matters." His wife wrapped her arm around his waist.

Valentina rolled her eyes and glanced back at Ryan, who stood there studying her. He opened his mouth as if to speak but then his phone rang.

"You're still here?" Roman tossed out as he led Madison past him.

"Fuck you, Caponelli," Ryan replied.

"As long as it's not my sister." Only the fact that the two had a long history allowed them to speak to one another that way. They'd probably said worse when they were on the football field together. It also hit home the fact that there was no use thinking about a future with the one she pined for such a long time. Their families and lives were too different and nothing would ever change that. It was time to stop any involvement before it started. Roman stopped and glanced at her. "Coming?"

"Uh, yes." She risked a quick look in Ryan's direction but he had answered the call and was deep in conversation. Obviously, something important had come up. He spoke in a hushed and serious tone, not focused on anything else. The evening had not turned out anything like she expected but it was too late now. There were still some things she wanted to say to Ryan but Roman and Madison expected her to join them. Family came first.

"Roman?" Ryan called out, and her brother turned.

"Keep an eye on her. I had to get rid of one jerk bugging her tonight. I don't want to worry about any others."

"Don't worry." Roman walked while he talked but stopped briefly to turn around and add, "Thanks." They both nodded and went their separate ways. The relationship her brother had with Ryan was just as complicated as the one she had with him.

Before going back in the bar, she noticed Ryan getting in a vehicle and driving off. The tires spun and dirt flew. Something must have happened. He was off duty, but was he ever off the job?

"Val, are you are all right?" Madison ushered her through the door.

"Yes, I'm fine." Her eyes took a moment to adjust to the dim lighting but it was nice to be in where it was warm.

"You don't look fine. Let's find a table and chat before Roman gets back." Her sister-in-law, already very much the mobster's wife, chose a spot in a dim corner and left the chair with the back to the wall for her husband. He'd be able to see everyone who came in and out.

"It was just a misunderstanding. I went to thank Officer Ryan for helping me and then he ended up kissing me." Val crossed her legs and swung her foot. "It was no big deal."

"The thanking part or the kiss?" Madison teased.

"The man infuriates me."

"Oh no. You've got it bad, girl."

"I do not." Valentina shook her head.

Madison spied her husband headed their way with a waitress trailing behind with a tray of drinks. "Tomorrow, you and me, I want all the details." They hushed up as soon as Roman came near.

"What'd I miss? Did lover boy finally leave?" He took the empty chair and the server left their drinks.

"Oh, Romeo." Valentina called him by the nickname he hated and only she was allowed to use.

"Don't *Romeo* me. I just don't want you to get hurt, and Caponellis and lawmen don't mix." He tapped his fingers on the table.

"How can you say that when I'm a lawyer? I'm part of the legal system."

"The only reason father ever paid for school and allowed you to become an attorney was to protect us from the law." He pointed a finger at her. "And don't ever forget it."

Valentina pouted and folded her arms across her chest.

"Okay, you two," Madison interrupted. "I've been looking forward to this all day. Let's change the subject and enjoy ourselves." Her companions both grumbled.

Valentina took a long sip of her drink. *Paid and allowed.* How dare he. When would she ever be able to live her own life? She sat up a little straighter. Her first step to independence was leaving Chicago. The second was opening her own office. The next would be to date who she wanted to date, not who she was allowed to, and tomorrow she would make that happen. There had to be someone who could take her mind off the drop dead sexy Ryan Donavan.

Ryan

The night turned even colder and Ryan grabbed a coat before rushing into the emergency room. Danny rose from a chair in the waiting room and was heading his way when he spied her. She'd phoned to say Tyler was in the hospital.

"What happened?"

"He's pretty scraped up but the doctors say he'll be fine."

"That's good, but what happened?" People needed to get to the point and not beat around the bush.

"Kid was riding home on his bike and got hit by a car. His room is down here." She led the way. "A woman spotted him lying by the side of the road and called it in. He refuses to talk to anyone. Doc said he'll probably be released in the morning. They're keeping him overnight for observation since he took a bad hit to the head."

"Do you think it might be gang related or anything like that?" Ryan kept a close eye on that and refused to let anything even linked to a gang into his town. The one good thing about a branch of the Caponelli crime family living in Genoa was that they didn't want gangs there either. Everyone knew Roman wouldn't tolerate illegal drugs of any kind in this town. *Never thought I would agree with the man on anything but I do on this.* Even the local motorcycle clubs kept illegal activities outside the county line.

"Could be." She frowned. "What would a kid be doing riding a bike this late? It's a school night. Where are his parents?"

Ryan sighed. "His father died a few years ago and his mom's working two jobs, maybe three."

She nodded. "Well, she sure doesn't need this added stress or more bills." Danny stopped outside Tyler's door.

"Let me talk to him and see what I can find out."

"Will do. I better get back to the station and finish my report." She didn't wait for a reply before heading back down the hallway.

He knocked lightly on the hospital room door.

"Yeah." The voice was weak but definitely Tyler's.

Ryan entered and pulled a chair close to the bed. The sight of Tyler battered and bruised hit him in the heart and the gut at the same time. It wasn't the kid's fault he grew up in the poor part of town without a father in the house. His mother did the best she could, but working long hours to keep a roof over their head left little time for proper supervision.

"So tell me what happened." Pain was written all over his black and blue face.

Tyler eyed him from head to toe. "What are you, a Texas Ranger now or something?"

"I got dragged away from a western party, and a very beautiful woman, I might add, so I'm in no mood for messing around."

"If you're not working, then why are you here?" He pulled his blanket higher and crossed his arms over his chest.

"Because I happen to care about the people in this town, and that includes you. I don't have time for any bullshit so tell me what happened."

Tyler turned his head away, his mouth set.

"Okay, I asked nicely, but now it's going to get tougher. Do I need to get social services involved?"

That caused the kid's pale face to go even whiter. "I was just trying to help." Tyler's voice cracked.

67

"Help do what?" Ryan inched his chair closer.

"I know how hard my mom works so I got a job at the gas station on the edge of town after hours." The young man fought back tears. "I was just trying to make some money to help out. I got run off the road, crashed my bike, and then didn't show up for my first night. I know I've screwed up in the past but now no one will hire me."

"Did you see who hit you? Did you get a license plate number?" A hit and run was serious.

"No." He shook his head and then winced. "What am I going to do? Now we will have more bills." The tough kid was near tears. "I was just trying to help. She needs money."

Ryan rested his elbows on his knees and rubbed his chin. He couldn't blame the kid for trying to help his mom, but sneaking out to work on a school night was definitely not the right way. He took a deep breath and leaned back in his chair.

"What if you'd been killed? Your mother would have been devastated. It's not safe being out after dark on a bike, especially this time of year."

"It was stupid, I know, but after I got caught shoplifting a few years ago I can't get a job to save my life."

"It's tough losing a parent." Ryan knew. He'd lost both on the same day and he'd been younger than Tyler at the time. The bouts of shoplifting and skipping school had probably been a product of the grief. It could have been so much worse. At least Tyler had stayed away from drugs and the gangs that had been here before the Caponellis took residence. "Here's what we're going to do. Let me see if we can get you into some kind of work program. Maybe there's something you can do at the station."

"Yes. I'll do anything. Sweep floors, take out the trash," Tyler offered.

"I can't promise anything, but I want you to promise me something." Ryan stared him straight in the eye.

Tyler nodded. "Yes, sir."

"No more sneaking out at night. Your mom has enough on her mind."

"I promise."

The chair legs squeaked as he stood up and slid it back toward the wall. Ryan placed a hand on the guardrail of the bed. "Rest up. If you need a ride home in the morning, give me a call." He pulled a card out of his pocket and set it on the table next to the bed.

"Thanks, I appreciate it, but my mom said she'd be back here in the morning. She had to go back to work."

"Where's she at now?"

Tyler told him about the late-night diner she waitressed at.

"I'll stop by and let her know I'll bring you home. We don't want her falling asleep and getting into an accident herself. Call me before they let you out."

Ryan tapped the card on the night stand and started for the door. "Get some sleep and I'll see what kind of work I can find for you."

"I'll do anything and I'll work hard." Tyler sat up in the bed too quickly and put his hand to his head again.

"We'll talk about that when you are better. Now, get some rest."

"I will."

Ryan turned off the light and left the room. He covered his yawn with his hand as he wandered down the empty hospital hall. A night nurse smiled as he walked by. The evening sure hadn't turned out as planned. That was for damn sure.

Cold, brisk air gave him a burst of energy as he exited the hospital. The automatic sliding doors closed fast as if fighting to keep the heat in place. Days like this made him feel old. Just a little over thirty years old and he was still going home alone.

Ryan hoped he could keep his promise to Tyler. It would be like pulling teeth to get employers to take a chance on a youngster with a checkered past. He could have turned out the same way. His mother and father had died tragically. There was no one there when Ryan returned home after school. Hours passed and it was dark by the time his uncle knocked on the door to tell him neither parent would be coming home again. Ever. He felt like a zombie as he packed up his things and followed Uncle Patrick out the door. It was then that he'd transferred schools and ended up in the private academy with Roman and Valentina. It was crazy how a few minutes, sometimes seconds, could change your entire life.

The truck's heater kicked in instantly. Ryan took the long way home, stopping in at the diner to assure Tyler's mom that he was resting fine and that he would bring him home in the morning. She protested at first but the woman was clearly exhausted and finally agreed. He then detoured past the bar he'd been at earlier. Remembering the kiss he'd shared with Valentina had him adjusting the temperature in the cab to cool. She was the one bright spot in his day, until her brother showed up and dimmed things. The prick. Not that he blamed him. If he had a sister, he'd be as watchful as Roman.

He'd not been making much headway with Valentina but he planned to make it up to her sometime soon. Ryan slowed and took a turn around the parking lot. Her truck was nowhere in sight. A chuckle escaped his lips thinking of her in that huge truck. He'd dropped off a squad car for an oil change just as she was driving out and the mechanic mentioned that the long-legged brunette just bought it. It wasn't any bigger than his but it surprised the hell out of him. She surprised the hell out of him. Pausing before turning into the street, he cursed and headed for the place he'd heard she'd moved to, or was moving to. It was a small town so he knew she'd been staying with her brother and Madison. It felt a bit stalkerish but he wanted to make sure the woman got home safe. He wanted all the residents of Lake Genoa to get home safe.

In mere minutes he cruised down her street and spotted her truck parked in the driveway of an old Victorian home. The lights were on and he spied her slim figure walk by the window. It took all he had not to stop and scold her for keeping her shades open at night and to double check that she'd locked her doors, but he'd probably come across as a peeping Tom. Knowing her brother, the place probably already had a kick-ass security system and was being monitored twenty-four seven.

He'd always thought of Valentina as being sheltered, a rich princess in a tower. Ryan had taken an oath to protect and serve, but at this moment in time, the only one he most wanted to save from harm was the one out of reach.

Chapter Eight

Valentina

Valentina yawned and rubbed her eyes as she studied her new office. It was nicely decorated in earth tones and a few lakeside photos dotted the walls. All she needed was the shingle with her name on it outside the door and she would be open for business. That sign was supposed to be on the door by the end of the day. It was a nice surprise when Madison greeted her first thing in the morning with treats from the Java Shop.

"That was fun last night." Madison sipped her latte and stuffed the last bite of a chocolate pastry in her mouth. They sat on opposite sides of her desk, still empty of paperwork and files.

"You sure are chipper today. How do you do it? It's like you're going nonstop all the time and you don't look a bit worse for wear." If there was a secret, she wanted to be let in on it.

"It's just love." Madison's cheeks flushed. "I know it's corny, but ever since I've been with

Roman, I wake up with a smile on my face each day."

Valentina rolled her eyes. "Ugh, you didn't grow up with him tormenting you every day and hiding your dolls. What a pest."

Her lovesick companion just laughed. "No, but I bet he never let anyone else torment you."

"You are correct on that one." Val took a long sip from her coffee and set the cup on the table. "You know it's not always going to be that way. Right?"

"Of course. That's why marriage vows include the phrase *for better or for worse.*"

"You know what I mean." Her sister-in-law knew she'd married into a mafia family but had no idea what it was like to grow up in one.

"Yes, I do know." Madison sobered. "I've witnessed more violence since I've known Roman than I have in my entire lifetime. But it was Roman who protected me and kept me and others safe. He also promised to move the family to more legit businesses and I believe him. It will take time, and I know to not ask any questions that I don't want to know the answers to."

"That's a start." Valentina frowned.

"What's wrong, girl?"

"I guess I just see everyone living their dreams, falling in love, reaching their goals." Her gaze wondered to the window.

"It looks to me like you are living your dream and reaching your goals." Madison leaned forward. "We're sitting in your new office. As soon as the sign is on the door, the place will be booming."

"I think I'm just worried about failing." Valentina turned in her chair.

"If you are worry about failing, you'll never do anything. I'm amazed at all you've done. You have no idea how much of a loser I feel like sometimes when I think of all you've accomplished. It's amazing." Madison was singing her praises

Valentina's cheeks flushed with the tribute. "Are you kidding me?"

"No. How many people your age have both a law office and a place like Firenza?"

Val shrugged and slumped back in her chair. It was a lot, but if it weren't for her family, she wouldn't have half of the things she had. It had been their money that had afforded her to do the things she'd done.

"But I don't think that is what has you in a funk. You want our handsome law enforcement officer for yourself, and don't try and deny it."

"So what if I do? He doesn't want me." She took another sip of her latte.

"How do you know?" Madison stood up and walked around the room as she talked. "I think you are both so uptight about what everyone thinks that you don't know what you want." Truer words could not have been spoken.

"Our family—" Val started, but was interrupted.

"I have a feeling that no matter who you pick for your man, Roman and your father are going to hate him." She stopped in front of the desk and placed her hands on her hips. "That said, I think Officer Ryan is the only one with enough balls to stand up to both of them. And if you like him as much as I think you do, you'd better go get him before someone else does."

"I just don't know." There was a knot in her gut.

"For a lawyer, you sure don't put up much of a fight."

"I'm a damn good fighter. I'm just not good as this dating stuff."

"Is anyone? Geez, girl. Do you like him?" Madison challenged.

"Yes." She lifted one shoulder and dropped it. "He's good looking."

"And?"

"He has a job and seems to care about people."

"And?"

"And I have no idea what to do about it."

"I do."

"What, walk over and ask him out?"

"No, but you could get to know him first. Looks are fine but you have to have something to back that up."

Of course looks faded, but it was his drive to always do what was right that appealed to her. After being in a family that always seemed to be on the wrong side of the law, someone on the right side was a step in the right direction.

"I agree, but I feel like I made a mess of everything the other night, not to mention big brother stepping in and threatening him."

"I don't think Ryan seemed too upset. I think he would have stayed if he hadn't gotten that phone call. It had to have been important for him to leave." Her sister-in-law crossed her arms over her chest and was quiet. After a few seconds, her face lit up.

"I know. I know what you could do."

"What?" Valentina would take any suggestions she could get. After all, Madison had snagged one of the most sought after and richest bachelors around.

"I ran into Danny the other day and she mentioned a new program they were starting at the station. It's for troubled kids and kids who just needed some direction. A type of work program to give them experience. You could go down to the station and sign your law office up. Just think, you could get someone to help around here. Make coffee, file papers, things like that." She stopped and made a sweeping motion with her hand. "Well, when you have some work."

A work program? Her chair creaked as she leaned back. That was a good idea to have someone here in case she had to leave. She would eventually need help. "I like it."

Madison rounded the desk and gave Val's chair a push. She was nothing if not subtle. "Go down there before you chicken out."

Grabbing her purse, Valentina got to her feet. "Let's go."

"Oh, hell no. You are doing this on your own."

"Okay." She tossed both of their empty coffee cups in the trash. "Well, can I at least give you a ride somewhere?"

They walked out the door and she spied Arlo leaning against one of Roman's black SUVs. "I forgot your ride is already here. Hi, Arlo." She waved and he nodded.

"Good luck, Val. My only advice is if it is meant

to be, it will be." Madison gave her a shoulder a quick squeeze.

"What's meant to be?" her brother's, and now Madison's, bodyguard asked as he opened the vehicle door.

"I'm trying to find Val a man," Maddy explained.

Arlo rolled his eyes. "Heaven help the poor man," he grumbled under his breath.

"What?" That hurt. Valentina pouted.

"I didn't mean it that way. You know I love ya like a sister, but you know what it's like with your brother and father. Have you ever even gone on a date?"

Val stopped and turned bright red. "Yes, a couple times, in fact."

"What?" Madison gasped. "You're joking, right?"

"There wasn't much time for fun." Never had she felt so stupid and she narrowed her eyes at Arlo, who whispered an apology.

"I'm so sorry. I didn't mean it that way." Madison touched her arm. "You'll be fine. He's a good man. I know it."

Confidence gone, Val hugged her goodbye and stepped back to the sidewalk. Shutting the door, Arlo stepped to her side. "For what it's worth, the man who will be able to stand up to your family will be the one I respect to stand by your side." He patted her shoulder before rounding the vehicle. Tears threatened. Arlo was a good man and just as single as she was, but like he said, they were like brother and sister. He started the SUV and the pair disappeared down the street.

A cool breeze caressed her cheek and Valentina hugged her sweater tighter. Soon, she wouldn't be able to be outside without a coat. The thought of spending another cold winter alone stiffened her resolve to find that special someone. Whether going to the local police department today would fix that problem remained to be seen. At least she was doing something good and hopefully help out a youth who needed direction.

She may have cursed her family at times but she had always been taken care of and protected. Not everyone was that lucky.

Ryan

Ryan eyed the box of donuts in the breakroom with caution. They looked good but it was hard to tell how long they'd been there. Using his better judgement, he just poured some coffee that was probably passed its freshness date as well. What it lacked in taste it made up for in temperature.

The hot liquid seemed to burn its way down his throat and his cheeks heated. It did the trick to clear the cobwebs in his brain. His usually quiet town was getting busy. In just a few short days there was a young woman's death, Tyler's accident, and, of course, the return of Valentina Caponelli. What was he thinking kissing her? She was trouble. It wasn't her fault but it was guilt by association. Still, it was worth it. The coffee warmed his belly, or was it his thoughts of a certain beauty from Chicago.

Walking out of the room, he thought he must be dreaming. Valentina was talking to Danny at the front desk. If Roman was standing with her, it would be a strong bet that she was there to file a sexual harassment charge for manhandling her in a parking lot, but she was by herself. She was also smiling, a beautiful, heart stopping smile. Her lips were full and soft. That he remembered and would never forget. He leaned to rest a shoulder against the wall, but quickly recovered after realizing he was a lot farther away than he thought. Except for some coffee spotting the floor, there was no damage done. Ryan quickly grabbed some napkins from the breakroom.

Mess cleaned up, he was ready to go say hi to Valentina, but she was gone.

"Hi, Ry," Danny greeted as she walked by.

"Hi." He grabbed her arm. "Uh, hey, Danny, got a sec?"

"Yeah, what's up? At least you are." She laughed. "I saw you almost wipe out. What the hell was that about?"

"Nothing. I slipped." He tried to brush it away. "Say, was that Miss Caponelli you were talking to?"

"Valentina?" She tilted her head and rested her elbows on her gun belt. "Are you serious? You've got it bad."

He rubbed his forehead. "Not sure what you mean."

"Yes, you do. Of course it was her. Damn, if you want to date her, just go ask her," she teased.

"I. Don't. Date." Saying it one word at a time wasn't fooling anyone but he tried. "I just wanted to know why she was here."

A fist came out of nowhere and hit him in the arm. "You know what, Donavan? You're a dumbass."

"Oww! What the hell, Danny?" He rubbed the sore spot. Not only did she swear worse than any man, she hit harder.

"I don't know the reasoning behind why you don't want to date, but in the right light you aren't half bad to look at. Do yourself, and the rest of us, a favor and go ask her out. You don't want to end up alone. You remember old man Halverson. Don't ya?"

How could he forget? That was a bad day, to say the least. John Halverson and his brother had been bachelors for years and lived on the edge of town. A few years ago, John's brother died, leaving him home alone, just him and his old Collie dog. One day they got a call at the station from Halverson's mailman. The box at the end of his driveway was full and the man's car hadn't moved in a week.

Ryan and Danny drove out to see what was going on. They could tell as soon as they looked in the window that the man was dead and had been for at least a week. It was a sad case. The poor dog was starved half to death and wouldn't let anyone near his master. To this day it still brought a tear to his eye.

"I don't want to end up like John." It choked him up just to speak about it.

"Then don't." She pointed a finger in his face. "I

81

like dicks, not chicks, and even I think she's hot. I could tell Valentina was looking around too. Like she was hoping to catch sight of you."

"You think so?" It would be easier if he knew she felt the same way but their time together the other night had been a disaster. "What was she doing here anyway?"

"Your love goddess was just wondering about the work program the department just started. She wants to hire someone for her law office."

"Really? I forgot about that." Not only did his admiration for her just go up a notch, his pride did too. It was a win-win situation. The program kept kids busy and off the street while giving them valuable work experience, and the company got much needed help.

"Really. Are we done now? Do you have your head out of your ass so I can get some work done?"

"Yeah." He couldn't help but laugh. Whoever ended up with Danny would have his hands full, that was for sure.

"I'm hoping to go over all the reports from Tracy's death. We should have the autopsy results soon." The woman was already stepping backward down the hallway.

"As soon as you hear anything, let me know." It still kicked him in the gut every time he thought of her dying at such a young age and all alone. The image would probably never be erased from his mind.

"Okay, well, I better see if I can catch up with Val, uh, Miss Caponelli and see what we can come up with."

Danny smiled. "Just bring her some flowers. Girls like that kind of shit."

"I'll do even better." The idea was already forming in his mind. "I'll bring her a kid."

Chapter Nine

"The doc said I should be resting." Tyler sat in the passenger seat, a frown on his face and his arms crossed. "I've got a headache."

"The doctor said you're fine. I thought you wanted a job. Would you rather I take you home?" That got his companion to shut his mouth. Ryan rested his elbow on the armrest. It seemed like a good idea at the time but now he was starting to question the whole idea. The last woman in the world he needed to be with was Valentina, yet she was the only one who got his blood flowing. Why was he going back and forth all the time?

If he could get the woman in his bed, maybe that would rid him of the obsession he had with her. Unfortunately, that would be an even worse idea. Roman would have his cleaner, Dominic, chop him up in little pieces and throw his body in the lake. Nope, that was not going to happen.

Nonetheless, here he was driving to her new office with the offering of a juvenile delinquent to brighten her day. Danny was right. He did have it bad, and it wasn't a good thing. Not many people knew the true history of his family, especially her, and that's the way it should remain. Valentina was his weakness. She was a woman who could cause a good man to go bad.

"Who is this chick anyway? Some butt ugly—"

The wheels screeched as Ryan slammed on the brakes. Luckily, they were on a side street and there was no traffic. "If I hear one more disrespectful word out of your mouth, I'm turning around and dropping you off at your mother's. Do you understand me?"

Tyler rolled his eyes. "Yes, sir."

"I thought you wanted a job." *Kids these days, if it wasn't one thing, it was ten dozen.*

"I do, but I don't know nothing about working for a lawyer. I break laws, I don't fix them. Besides, she's probably going to look down on me just like the rest."

That Tyler trusted him enough to tell him his concerns was a start. Apparently, Tyler was just as scared about meeting Valentina as Ryan was about asking her out. The kid lacked confidence and it had been rough on him growing up without a father or any strong male role models in his life. "You don't have to worry about that. Miss Caponelli requested someone just like you." He eased the vehicle back down the road again.

"What do you mean, someone like me?" Tyler asked. "A charity case, a loser, a—"

Ryan wheeled the squad car along the curb and put it in park. "No, she just wants to help." He turned to face Tyler but the kid was staring out the windshield. "What's wrong now?"

"Nothing. Wow, she's beautiful." He pointed up ahead.

It was Valentina, and she was in full Miss Caponelli attire. She wore sky high black heels with those red soles, a short, tight, dark skirt, and a burgundy sweater. "That's your new butt ugly boss."

"Are kidding me?" It was hard to judge the expression on his face. It was a cross between awe and fear.

"Nope, and I do not want to hear one word of you disrespecting her or you will be gone in two seconds flat." He unbuckled his seatbelt and got out of the car.

"Yes, sir." Tyler seemed to be a little more agreeable about things now and soon joined him on the sidewalk. That was until fear marked his face and the kid grabbed his arm.

"What's wrong now?" Ryan looked around.

"Don't you know who that is?" he gasped.

"Valentina? Of course."

"No, I mean the guy next to her. He's a killer. You'd better get your gun out. Now." The kid ducked behind him.

Valentina stood watching a long-haired man as he installed an intricate iron railing to her new handicap ramp. It was Dominic—the guy who came in and made any mess, no matter how bloody, disappear. There was no proof of anything. The guy was the best at what he did, but it was still rumored that was what he did. "Relax. He works for her brother." It was easier said than done. The guy even creeped him out but he would never hurt Valentina.

"Her brother?" Tyler starred up at the red leaves on a nearby maple tree.

"You got a problem with that?" What was the kid thinking now?

"I guess not. You aren't having me secretly killed, are you?" He peeked up at him.

Ryan placed a hand on the youngster's shoulder. "No, if I was going to do that, I'd let you know." He winked and guided him by the arm in Val and Dom's direction.

Valentina turned their way and shaded her eyes with her hand. A hesitant smile lit up her face and Ryan's steps slowed. Tyler smirked and slipped from his gasp. "You've got the hots for her, don't you?"

"No, our relationship is strictly professional." But, oh, how he wished that would change.

"Yeah, right." Tyler shook his head.

"Morning, Valentina," Ryan said, and Tyler bumped him with his elbow. Obviously, the kid was more observant than he thought.

She stepped forward and greeted them. "Officer Ryan. To what do we owe this unexpected surprise?"

He noticed both Dom and Tyler glancing back and forth between him and Val. "Got a proposition for you."

Val's eyes widened and she blushed.

"This your new office?" He knew it was but it seemed like whenever she was around, the words came out all wrong.

"Yes, just put up the shingle today." She pointed

to her new sign. **'*Valentina Caponelli, Attorney at Law.*'**

Her handyman came and stood next to her, a hammer in one hand and a threatening expression on his face.

"Dominic." Ryan glanced at the railing. "Looks like the place is coming along great. When is opening day?"

"If I can get the ad in the paper this afternoon, I hope for Monday. Who do you have here?"

"This is Tyler Wilson."

She offered him her slender hand. Even her hand was elegant with her red nails and slim fingers. "Tyler. It's a pleasure to meet you." He shook her hand without pause. Gone was the snarky kid from the car. He seemed to be in awe of her.

"I heard at the station that you were looking for someone to mentor and I brought Ty here in that hopes that we could work something out."

"That's wonderful. Come on in." She motioned for them to follow. "I'll make some coffee and we'll chat."

Dominic grabbed her arm and spoke a few words in Italian. Color sparked her cheeks and she shook her head, brushing him off. "Whatever, you can go get some if you want."

"I'm just warning you," was his response, and he went over to continue his work.

They followed her up the stairs and into her new law office. It was hard not to stare at her sleek calves and ankles. If he wasn't a leg man before, he was now. Ryan stepped in front of her and opened the door.

"Ladies first."

"Thank you."

Tyler shook his head at Ryan and followed behind.

"Would either of you like some coffee?" Tyler answered yes but Ryan declined. She poured the kid a cup and handed to him. "There's sugar and creamer in the fridge if you like."

"Thanks, Miss Caponelli." He grinned and was either as taken with her as he was or scared that her brother would have the handyman cut him into little pieces.

"At least someone trusts my coffee making skills." She marched over to Ryan. "Don't tell me you speak Italian and heard what Dom said." Her fists clenched.

"No, I'm afraid not, but now you've got me wondering."

She shrugged. "It's a long-standing joke in my family that I make the worst coffee possible. Dominic was just reminding me that it wouldn't be a good idea to poison a cop."

Ryan's eyes met Tyler's as the kid sniffed what was in his cup before he poured half into the sink.

Valentina twisted to see where he was looking. "It's not that bad, is it?"

Tyler shook his head and showed her his cup. "No. See, half gone already."

"Wonderful. There's more, so help yourself."

The poor kid's eyes were huge and met Ryan's again across the room.

"Well, thank you for your hospitality but he's not here to socialize. You said you needed some help around here."

"Yes, of course, please take a seat." She motioned them over to a seating area. Her office space was small but seemed the perfect size for a solitary lawyer. It was just a waiting area complete with a small counter with coffee and a small fridge with bottled water. There was a burgundy-colored couch, two tan side chairs, and a coffee table in the center with the local newspaper and a few magazines on top. There were a few photos of the lake on the walls. He'd not seen her office but it was a good bet that was equally as nice.

Valentina sat in one chair and crossed her ankles to the side. He took the one opposite and Tyler settled down on the couch and placed his empty cup on the table. Spying it, Valentina jumped to her feet. "Can I get you another?"

"Oh, no. Thanks. I'll be up all night if I drink too much." Tyler turned toward Ryan, as if asking for help. It was all he could do not to laugh. The kid tried his hardest to come across as a badass, yet not wanting to disappoint a mob boss's daughter struck fear into his heart.

"Okay." She sat down. "If there is anything else I can get you, just let me know."

"Thank you. I came here to get a job," Tyler said, encouraging her to get back on track.

"Yes. I need someone to help out. Someone to run errands, greet clients, help clean up the place. Does that sound like something you would like to do?"

"How much does it pay?" the kid asked.

"Hey," Ryan interrupted. "You should be happy

to get the experience." He knew she would pay him but it seemed rude to ask up front.

"I'm happy to pay you and give you experience." She told him a wage that was quite a bit more than either expected. "Have you ever been interested in becoming a lawyer?"

"Me? Oh, hell no." Tyler laughed. "I mean, no."

"Tyler here has unfortunately been walking the line between the right side and the wrong side of the law. We are hoping that you might be a good influence and he'll gain some valuable work experience."

"Believe me, with my family, that is a situation I can relate to," she said, trying to put Tyler at ease.

"I'll work hard," the kid added.

"I'm sure you will. When can you start?" Valentina asked.

Tyler turned Ryan's way before finally answering, "I guess anytime."

"How about today?"

"Sure. I guess so."

"He's not in school today but he will need to work after school hours or on the weekend."

She nodded. "Of course."

A bell over the front door jingled as Dominic came in carrying a box with a bow on top. Ryan had to fight the grin when he saw it contained one of those single serve coffee makers.

"Where'd that come from?" Valentina tapped her finger on the arm of the chair.

"Gift," he grumbled before dropping it on the counter and then leaving by the same door. Her face turned bright red. Obviously, her handyman was a complex man. Was the gift for her or her customers?

Tyler broke the silence. "My mom wants one of those."

"Well, you can—" Val started before Ryan held up his hand and interrupted.

"That's the good thing about having a job. You can save up your money and surprise her with one. Wouldn't that be a nice thing? Especially knowing that you earned it the right way." The last thing he wanted was for her to just give Tyler everything. He had to learn to accomplish things on his own and the value of hard work. It would be so easy for her to spoil the boy. Even though she came from a cruel family, he knew she was a kind-hearted person.

"Yeah. She'd like that," Tyler agreed.

Ryan got to his feet. "Well, Val." The use of her name seemed to soften her expression after being rudely interrupted. "I better get going." What was the point of staying around and trying to put the moves on her when they were surrounded by her employees?

Dominic came in again, this time carrying a lamp.

"Dom," Valentina also stood, "this is Tyler. I just hired him to help out around here. Why don't you have him help you carry in all those files?"

A man of few words, the guy just motioned for the kid to follow and they both left the room.

"Thanks again for taking him under your wing. He's had a rough time of it lately."

Her beautiful eyes glanced up at him. She now stood so close her perfume drew him nearer. It was sweet and spicy, just like the woman herself. Her lips parted and her eyes widened.

"I'm so sorry to hear that. I know he mentioned his mother, but where is his father?"

"He was killed in a car accident, and if anyone knows how hard it is to grow up without a dad in your life, that would be me."

She bit her lip and her gaze dropped to floor before shifting to the door. "Well, I don't want to keep you." She rushed to open it, giving him no choice but to leave. "Thanks again. We will give Tyler a ride home." And then the door was slammed in his face. What the hell? Did he misinterpret that knee shaking kiss?

His gaze drifted back and forth between the entrance to her office and his car. That didn't go as planned, but hopefully it would work out well for both Valentina and Tyler, and that was the most important thing. Ryan studied the unlikely duo of Dominic and Ty carrying some law books inside before striding to his vehicle. He had the door halfway open when the ring of his cell phone sounded.

"Donavan."

"Ry." It was Danny. "We've got another one."

"Another what?"

"Another dead body."

Chapter Ten

Valentina

"Uh...thanks." Valentina sat on the couch in the waiting room of her new office and tossed the wrapping paper to the side. "A person can never have too many coffeemakers." It was the third one today. First was the one from Dominic, then Arlo stopped by with one, and now Roman and Madison had just gifted her one along with ten cases of single serve gourmet coffees. The gesture was grand yet a little insulting at the same time. Her lips pouted. "Am I really that bad at making coffee?"

"Yes," her brother answered.

"Roman." Madison punched her husband in the arm. "That wasn't very nice."

"It's the truth and you know it. Sorry, sis, but you can't do anything in the kitchen to save your life."

"What?" Her shoulders sank. How could he say such a thing? "I'm a great cook."

"Roman!" Madison stomped her foot and waved

her hands in the air.

"Who gives a shit if you can or can't cook? I certainly don't." He took a seat on her desk.

"I'm a lawyer, but I can't make coffee."

"This isn't the fifties. Do you think it would matter to me if Madison couldn't cook? Her other skills more than make up for that." He winked at his wife and she turned bright red. "Marry a fireman. They can all cook."

"Stop it. I can cook. Besides, you know Father would have a fit about that."

"He'd get over it."

"When hell froze over maybe."

"You don't need a man anyway." Roman crossed his arms across his chest. "You've got all of us. Arlo, Dom, all the guys."

As if that made her lack of dating any better. Her hormones must have really been out of whack. She'd never been this needy before. Or course, she'd never had this much time on her hands before. School had been demanding and Roman and Madison had been running Firenza for so long, she wasn't needed there at all. That was going to change.

"Unfortunately, there are just some things I can't get from you and the guys."

"It will happen when you least expect it." Madison placed a hand on her shoulder. "You never know when you might toss some coffee on the man of your dreams." Madison and Roman had met at a coffee shop when she turned around and spilled hot latte all over one of his expensive shirts. Those two lovesick puppies actually kept showing up at the same place several days later hoping to catch each other, eventually sharing their first dance at the Snowflake Ball.

"Miss Caponelli, where do you want this?" Tyler entered the room carrying her framed law diploma in his hands.

"Have Dom hang it behind my desk in the office."

"He knows that but said to ask you before he puts a hundred nails in the wall."

"All right." She got to her feet. "Tell him I'll be right there." He turned to leave. "And, Tyler, I told you call me Val or Valentina. No Miss Caponelli here, okay?"

"Yes, Miss Cap—" he shook his head, "—I mean Valentina." The kid flashed her a bright smile before leaving the room.

"Who's that?" Roman motioned with his thumb.

"I was at the station today looking for kids to mentor and Ryan brought him over."

Madison grinned and Roman frowned.

"That still doesn't answer the question. Who is he and where does he live?"

"Oh my god. Roman. This isn't Chicago. If Ryan says he's okay to have around the place, I believe him."

"But if he is known around the station as needing special attention, there is obviously a reason. Did he get caught stealing or dealing drugs?" His face was set in a frown.

"Roman, hush. He might hear you." She held a finger to her lips. "I really don't know what his story is. Just that he needed a job. Something about his father being killed and his mom needed help with the bills. He seems like a nice young man."

"Well, get me his last name and I'll have Arlo check him out. If he and his family truly need help, we will see what we can do." She gave him Tyler's full name and her heart softened. Roman may have been a thorn in her backside at times with his over protectiveness, but he was also known to lend a hand to anyone who needed it. His phone buzzed and his face darkened when he read the message.

"I've got to go." He got to his feet and locked eyes with Dominic, who was on the other side of the room hooking up a flat screen television to the wall.

"Is something wrong?" Madison also rose.

"Nothing for you two to worry about. Maddy, you stay here and I'll be back soon. Dom, I need a word with you outside." The man put down his tools and followed him.

"Well, that was weird," Madison said, and rushed over to the window. "I didn't even get a kiss goodbye. Either the honeymoon phase is over or something big just went down."

"I'm thinking the latter." Their faces were so close to the window it fogged up. "And Dom's coming back inside instead of going with him." They turned to face each other after witnessing Roman get in the SUV with Arlo and head off down the street. "I don't like this at all. What do you think is up?"

"I don't know, but I'm not going to give up until someone gives me an answer." They both rushed to the man who'd just come in the door.

It took a while of nonstop pestering to get Dominic to crack but he did. Valentina didn't know all of his history but she did know he'd been tortured and abused. The fact that he often gave in to her demands meant he had a soft spot for her.

"What do you mean, ask my lover boy?" She tilted her head and crossed her arms in front of her chest.

"You know that badge that was here earlier." He brushed a piece of long hair behind his ear. For being so scary, the man was drop dead gorgeous. Dominic was from the old country, as made obvious by his slight accent. His skin always had that sun kissed tan to it and his long dark hair was the envy of any woman.

"That badge is not my lover boy." Although she wasn't opposed to that happening, she wasn't going to admit it. "If you don't tell me right now, I will call Roman and ask him. It must be important so I'm sure he won't want me bothering him."

Dominic took a deep breath and placed the hammer he had in his hands on a nearby counter. "There's been another death of a young woman. It's looking like Genoa might have a killer on the loose. Roman went to find out more."

"What?" Madison gasped and covered her mouth with her hand. "Things like that don't happen here."

"Bad things can happen anywhere."

"I know, but this is one of the reasons I left Chicago, and this is my new home." Valentina's face was white. "I just can't even imagine." She hugged herself. "Wait. Who was murdered?"

Valentina said a silent prayer as she did a visual

count in her head of all the good people she had met since moving to Genoa. Thinking that any one of them could be a victim made her sick to her stomach.

"I don't know." Dom leaned against the wall. "But I am not to let either one of you out of my sight until Roman is back."

Valentina glanced in her sister-in-law's direction and met her gaze. Both were very stubborn women, but right now neither wanted to test Roman's instructions, at least not until they knew all the details. The news had put her on edge. If there was a killer on the loose, that would be the last person she wanted to run into. "Where's Tyler?"

"I sent him to get us some lunch."

She was on the verge of pulling her hair out when the kid finally walked in the door, his arms loaded down with sandwiches, pasta, and drinks from the kitchen of Firenza. "Wow, what a cool place. I can't believe you own that," Tyler said, in awe of her other business. "Are you hiring?"

"You want another job?" Valentina started to unpack their meal.

"No, I think I will be very happy here. I was just thinking about my mom." He set the box of food on the coffee table.

"I thought she had a job."

"She does, but it's at a bar and she works really late hours." He tapped his toe a couple times against the leg of a chair. "I think it would be safer for her somewhere else."

He had her at the word safe, especially if the rumor of a possible killer of women in the area was true. "Let me make a call and we will see what we can do." Even if they didn't need extra help, she was getting Tyler's mom in. She couldn't bear the thought of something happening to her when Valentina could get her work somewhere safer. The security at Firenza was first rate. It had to be in their business. She stepped into her office and her fingers flew across the laptop as she sent off an email to her human resource person.

Her thoughts turned to Ryan. Law enforcement was a dangerous business, even more so today, but it really hit home now. Did she want to get involved with someone who might not come home at night? For some reason that didn't deter her from considering him as a potential romantic partner. She'd spent her whole life with the scary thought of many of her family members not returning at night—and some hadn't.

"I better call Ryan and see what I can find out." Not knowing what was going on was making her jittery.

"Leave him be. If he's in the middle of an investigation, the last thing we want to do is bother him." Madison had grabbed a to-go container and stuck her fork into some spaghetti. "I'm sure we will hear from Roman soon. That was where he was going, right?" She pointed her fork at Dom.

"Yeah, he's hoping to find out what happened and see what we can do to catch the bastard." It was no secret that Dominic loved to get rid of men who harmed others, especially women or children. In medieval times, he'd have been an executioner attired in black robes and a hood. Today, he was in a pair of tight jeans, work boots, and a long-sleeve tee.

"Catch who?" Tyler asked. "Did I miss something?"

"We just heard that there was a murder," Val informed him.

"We don't know for sure. Let's not panic." Madison was the voice of reason.

Tyler whipped out his phone and sent a text.

"Who are you texting?"

"My mom. The girl who died the other day lived next to our house."

"What?" Her jaw dropped. That was way too close. Not only was she going to get his mom a job, she would find them a new place to live.

"Yes, she was our neighbor. Nice lady." Tyler visibly relaxed when a text came back from his mother.

"This was in another area of town. At least that was where Roman and Arlo were headed." Dominic was usually the quiet one but the thirst for blood had him in a rather talkative mood. "I'll text Arlo and see what I can find out."

"I don't like this. I don't like this at all." Madison left half the food on her plate and started to pace. "Stuff like this doesn't happen here."

"Damn tourists from Chicago," Tyler muttered under his breath.

"I'm from Chicago and so is Officer Ryan," Valentina interjected.

"You're not tourists. You live here."

"Until we know more, I don't think we should speculate." Despite Madison trying to calm the group down, she kept walking back and forth. "I'm glad my mother and father are on vacation right now so I don't have to worry about them." After being separated for years, they'd been reunited, newly married, and traveling the world ever since.

"No one would dare harm you." The tone with which Tyler said it had Dominic glaring at him. "Well, it's true. She has bodyguards and is married to the biggest badass town. It's the rest of us who have to worry about getting killed."

"It's doesn't matter who you are." Dominic's voice was cold. "If someone wants to kill you bad enough, they will find a way." He picked up the hammer again. "I know, I've done it."

Chapter Eleven

This was the second time in less than a week Ryan was standing over a dead body, this time in the back room of a laundromat. It was not something a person wanted to get used to. Everything was the same and yet it was different. This was murder. This was planned. The victim was a mess.

The name on her pink smock said Amy. From the looks of the office, she didn't go down without a fight. There were chairs tipped over and spots of blood smeared on just about every surface. Her body was a crumpled heap on the floor. Her blonde hair was a mixture of red and white strands.

"Looks like trauma to the head again." Were Tracy and Amy somehow connected?

Danny's gloved finger pointed to a broken stapler lying on the floor. "Death by stapler? I don't think so, but there was definitely a struggle." Pen, paper, and even the contents of a trash can were lying about the room. It was messed up no matter what way you looked at it.

"It was more likely this." She picked up a heavy cast iron item next to the stapler. It had some blood and hair on it.

"What the hell is that?" Ryan asked.

"Obviously, you don't know antiques." Danny held it by the handle. "It's called a sad iron. They heat it on the stove and then use it to press clothes. It must have been a knickknack or paperweight on the desk."

"This is fucked up." Ryan squatted next to the victim as Danny continued to take photos from every angle.

"That's for damn sure." She snapped a few more shots. "How long do you think she's been like this?"

"From the condition and temperature of the body, I would say maybe late last night, early this morning." The coroner jotted down some notes. The vet had arrived at the same time he had. "This is one of those twenty-four-hour places. She could have been in the back about to lock up the office and been hit from behind."

Ryan glanced inside the store's open safe. "No money seems to be missing. So robbery is out." The deposit bag was still sitting there full of money, leaving him to believe she'd just unlocked the safe before being attacked.

"Tuesday, huh?" Danny stopped taking pictures and carefully shifted through a stack of items on the floor with her glove covered hands.

"You got something, Dan?" She was new to the force but Ryan already respected her keen senses. Danny often saw things the guys missed.

"It makes me think of those old towels."

"Towels?"

"My grandma had them."

Ryan raised an eyebrow. "Go on." The coroner was also listening.

"Monday was wash day. Tuesday was for ironing. Wednesday was for something else. Could be a coincidence, but just made me think of it. Tracy had a basket of laundry on the floor. We have an iron in a laundromat. I'm sure you can find some reproductions of the towels at a store. Let me check." She dug her phone out and did a search. When she found the right image, Danny handed it to him. Sure enough, there was an activity for each day of the week embroidered on flour sacks. Wednesday was mending day.

"Did you find any of those images here?"

"Not yet, but I will search the list for the other crime scene and see if there was anything there."

"Interesting, but what does it tell you about the killer?" the coroner questioned.

"Your guess is as good as mine. They hate housework? Who knows?" He was used to drunk and disorderly calls, not murders. "Danny, do a search of similar crimes and see if anything comes up. Also see if Tracy and Amy knew each other."

"Got it." She'd been jotting down notes and clicked her pen and put it in her pocket. "Anything else?"

"Nope, just get copies of the photos printed and wait for the others to get here. Does the victim have any next of kin?"

"I checked her phone for an ICE but nothing." It

always surprised him how many people failed to designate someone as their in case of emergency contact on their phone.

"Look at this." The coroner lifted the collar of the victim's smock. "It's some kind of puncture wound." It was as if someone had tried to stab her once, it didn't take, so they stabbed her again.

"Donavan?"

Ryan jumped when he heard his name being yelled from the other room. He recognized it as Roman Caponelli. Just what he needed. The guy probably wanted to chew him a new one for visiting his sister. The tall Italian in a suit strolled into the room.

"This is a crime scene. You shouldn't be in here."

"I had them add me to the list." He said it as if he was on the police payroll.

"You have no right to be on the list." Ryan glared at the new recruit at the door who meekly held a clipboard. Whenever there was a crime scene, they kept a list of everyone who came in so they could either add or delete people's DNA that might pop up in any test results.

Roman approached him so that they were out of anyone's earshot. "I want to know if there is anything I can do to help. Word is this might be a serial killer. We might be able to hunt them down and take care of the problem if you know who it is."

Just what he needed, a mafia posse out to take down a desperado.

"As much as I would love to have you hunt down and dispose of the problem, I don't know who it is. Plus, Caponelli, I am an officer of the law, and things don't work that way."

"Look, you know and I know that sometimes these bastards slip through the cracks. I have a wife and a sister here and I want this guy caught before anyone else gets hurt."

"And I don't want him caught?" The nerve of this guy thinking that the police weren't doing their jobs. These things took time. "The last thing we need is you going off and taking out the wrong person. Then where would we be?"

Roman turned his attention to the body on the floor and his jaw twitched. "What the hell? She's so young."

Grabbing him by the elbow, Ryan led him out the door. "And so was the other one. You can't tell anyone what you saw here. If word gets out, we could have copycat murders and god only knows what else." Police often kept a few clues from the scene from being public knowledge, something that in an interrogation only the true killer would know.

Tugging loose from his hold, Roman faced him. "I only let you lead me out of there because I know you have to show that you're in charge and I wasn't supposed to be in there, but if you ever put your hands on me again, you'll be shooting left handed."

"Are you threatening an officer?"

"No, I'm threatening Ry, the kid I went to high school with." Roman stepped back and smoothed his hair back with his hand. "You know I've got connections. If there is anything I can do to rid this town and the earth of the monster that did this, you let me know."

"There is. The other woman, Tracy, had a name in her appointment book, A. Man. Does that mean anything to you? Any mob men around we don't know about or anyone with that name?"

"Not that I can think of but I'll get some men on it. See if there is anyone who shouldn't be here."

An ambulance pulled up to the curb. Amy would be going for an autopsy and Danny would be riding with her to keep the chain of evidence intact. Hopefully, something would show up that might give a clue to not only her death, but Tracy's as well.

"In the meantime, have someone with Madison and Valentina at all times. We don't know who we're dealing with here," Ryan instructed.

They were quiet a moment as they nodded a greeting to the ambulance crew that walked by.

"Believe me, Madison will not be leaving my sight, and I'll have Dominic camp out at Val's place."

Ryan stiffened. "Are you sure you can trust him? The guy's a killer. I don't like him being anywhere near her."

"It doesn't matter what you think. I trust him with my life and hers."

"But I don't. I will be upping patrols. I have to stop by later to get Tyler anyway."

"Speaking of which. How do I know I can trust that kid?"

"He's a good kid, just going through a rough patch that I'd like to get smoothed out. I think it would be good for him to have a job, and Val needs the help."

"If she needs any help, any help at all, she just has to ask me."

"Maybe she wants some independence from the family."

"There is no getting away from the family, and we protect our own. I won't turn down the added security. We have cameras on all our residences and businesses so I'll have extra eyes on those as well." Roman and he may not have agreed on how things got done, but Ryan knew they both cared about keeping the people of their small town safe. "I want this murderer brought down, and fast."

"Finally something we can agree on. Just don't go off halfcocked. I don't need any more bodies in my town."

"It's my town too," Roman added.

"Then let's agree to keep it safe." Ryan held out his hand.

"Agreed. Keep in touch." Roman shook the offered hand and headed off to the black SUV. His always present bodyguard, Arlo, opened the door for him. The guy was the size of a linebacker. It just reaffirmed how different Valentina's life was from his. There were no cameras at his house, no bodyguards, and no family to protect him.

Ryan returned to the crime scene and greeted the ambulance guys that he'd met during car accidents and other scenes they were both at.

The first guy whistled and spoke before getting down to the business of getting the body onto the gurney. "Poor thing. I've got a daughter this age."

"You ever seen anything like this before?" Ryan asked from the doorway.

"In Genoa? The answer is no. When I lived in the big city, yes." The man shared a few stories of bizarre crime scenes he'd been to. The urge to get to Valentina's side was stronger than ever. He was thankful for her around-the-clock protection, but that wouldn't necessarily stop someone intent on killing.

He spied Danny scrolling through her phone again and her face lit up.

"Got something?" Ryan stepped to her side.

"I found one of those day of the week towels under the desk. I also did a search and you can buy towels like that at a place here in town." She held up the phone.

"No shit? Where?" He was eager to find this killer.

"Lakeside Commons. That new antique store. They sell both new and old stuff. You know, reproductions and such."

His stomach dropped. "That's where Valentina Caponelli just opened her new office."

"Do you want me to go check it out for you?" she offered.

"I think we both should. You go in normal clothes as a customer and I will go in my uniform. See what you can find out. Why did they just open here, where did the owners come from? We'll see if we each get the same answer."

"Will do. I'll go back to the station and change. See if I can find a towel in the list of Tracy's belongings that we might have missed."

"Thanks. Let me know what you find out."

"You got it." She started down the row of

washers and then stopped and turned around. "You should probably go make sure Valentina is okay. You know, with a potential killer possibly next door."

"We don't know that." He tried to brush it off but she was all he could think about.

"She doesn't know that either. Might score some points for you."

"I have a feeling you're trying to fix me up with her."

"No, just trying to protect the citizens of the town from your bad disposition." She winked. Was he really turning into a grumpy old man?

"I do have to pick up Tyler."

"Ry, just a suggestion. Women like flowers and candy." She shook her head, as if realizing he was a hopeless case. "Dropping off a juvenile delinquent never got anyone laid."

"Are you saying my skills with women are off? Why, I'm crushed." He placed a hand on his heart.

"It would take a lot more than words to crush you. You know you like her, I know you like her. Ask her out."

"No, I don't think so." He didn't do well in relationships. It was already becoming apparent that he was married to the job. Still, his heart wanted her.

"Scared she'll say no?" Danny taunted.

"No, afraid she'll say yes." The conflicts of interest alone were a mess. The town cop dating a mob princess.

"I never figured you for a chicken." She was not giving up.

"I'm not chicken, just smart enough to stay far from that family."

"From what I've seen, she wants to stay far from the family business as well." She flapped her arms a couple times like she was a chicken and then rushed out the door.

The last thing he'd ever be considered would be a coward, but he wanted to be smart. One needed to be careful about getting involved with the Caponelli family. Being a cop meant he had to be careful every day, but maybe it was time his personal life wasn't.

That was easier said than done. It was late afternoon by the time Ryan finally returned to the office of Valentina Caponelli. The new shiny gold sign glimmered on the wall next to the door. He tried the door but it was locked. Spying through the window, he noticed the place was empty. Even Tyler was nowhere to be found. Where was everyone?

Ryan turned to leave and take a look around back, but a scream from inside the building stopped him in his tracks.

Chapter Twelve

Valentina

The place was empty and way too quiet. Roman had picked up Madison and Dominic took Tyler home. She strolled from room to room. Her new office looked great but something was missing. Her lips tightened as studied the area.

The waiting room was perfect. Her private office was where things were lacking. Yes, it had the professional look, that was for sure, but it needed something. Her law books lined the shelves. A few green plants and ferns sat by the window. Valentina's gaze darted back to the bookcase. There were no personal effects. Having photos of her infamous family members would not be a good idea. Her clients would spend more time asking questions about them than telling about their cases.

She needed a hobby or something. Maybe earn a few trophies to put on her desk. But when would she have time for that? Valentina shook her head.

There was no time to do anything fun. A mental list of all the things she needed to do tomorrow floated through her mind. There were ads to be put in the paper, a website to design, flyers to put up around town, and so much more.

Val glanced at her watch. What was taking Dom so long? She arched her sore back and stretched her neck. It had been a long day. Her gaze landed on her framed diploma that still sat on the floor.

"I might as well get that hung up before he returns." Leaning against the wall, she slipped her feet out of the four-inch high stilettoes. With the frame in one hand, Valentina wheeled her new desk chair over to the wall. When she stepped up on the chair, she paused. Was that a knock at the door? She waited a moment but didn't hear the noise again. After a few minutes of struggling to find the nail with the wire on the back of the frame, her degree was finally on the wall.

Her head titled and then straightened. It appeared to be lined up right. With a hand on each side of the frame, she pushed the chair back to get a better look. Unfortunately, she pushed too hard and the wheels kept going.

"Help!" she screamed. The chair hit the desk and down she went with a big crash onto the floor. "Oww." Valentina carefully sat up and took a moment to catch her breath. Except for a sore forearm, she seemed to be okay.

A loud crash of breaking glass screeched from the other room.

"What the…?" She grabbed her purse, rolled behind the desk, and pulled a gun from her handbag's side pocket. Her heart pounded. What if it was the killer they'd talked about and he'd just broken into her place?

Her fingers shook as she held the gun in one hand and quickly crawled to the doorway. There was no way she would go down without a fight. She was a Caponelli, and Caponellis didn't run from anything. Well, except for handsome police officers who had the potential to break her heart.

The footsteps in the other room made the floor creak with every move. He, or she, was getting closer. It had to be a he—the footsteps sounded too heavy.

"Valentina?" a deep voice half whispered. It sounded familiar, but in her near panicked state it was hard to tell. Where the hell was Dominic? "Police. Come out with your hands up." Her ears perked up. It was Ryan, it had to be. But why the broken glass?

"Ryan?" She jumped to her feet and rushed from the room. She came to a halt when she realized his gun was pointed right at her. He motioned her to the side and poked his head into the office. "What's going on? Is the killer here?"

"You tell me. I heard you scream and had to break in." He continued to search all areas, including closets and the bathroom, before putting his gun away. "You got a permit for that?" He motioned to the gun in her hand.

How quickly she'd forgotten she still held it. "Of course I do, and my conceal carry permit too. Do you want to see it?"

"No, just put it away."

She found her purse on the floor where she'd left it, put the gun back in its holster, and returned to the front room.

"Hey. Wait a minute, you broke in?" Her stomach dropped when she spotted all the broken glass from her front door.

"Yeah. I knocked a couple times but you didn't answer. Then I heard you scream and thought someone was hurting you."

"I was hanging a picture and fell off the chair."

He took a step closer. "You fell? Are you all right? Do you need to go see a doctor?"

"Heavens no, but I do need a doctor for this door." Valentina grabbed a broom from the utility closet and started to sweep up the mess. It was the only noise in the room.

"I'm sorry about that. Let me clean up and I'll pay for the damages."

"No need. You were just trying to protect me." Her face heated as she looked his way. "I appreciate it."

"You know me. Officer Ryan, here to serve and protect." He took his hat off. "And destroy windows and doors." A mixture of emotions crossed his face. "I'm really sorry about that."

"No need to be." She stopped and rested her uninjured arm on the top of the broom. "I have to admit I was getting a bit apprehensive about being here by myself. Roman hasn't had the security cameras installed yet."

Surprise appeared on Ryan's face as he glanced around the room again. "I came to pick up Tyler. Where is he and your long-haired guard dog?"

"If you're talking about Dom, he took Tyler home. When we heard about the murder, he got worried about his mother. I wanted to make sure they were both home safe and sound before I left here. They might have had to wait a bit for his mom."

"I can't believe he left you here alone." Ryan flexed his fists.

"I can be very persuasive." She smiled.

"I can believe that, but still. I know Roman." He would be furious once he found out she'd been left alone against his orders.

"I promised to keep all the doors locked and not leave until he returned. I have a gun too."

Ryan chuckled. "I noticed." He took a deep breath. "So, what did you hear about the murder?"

"Not much but enough to be worried. I'm getting Tyler's mom a job at Firenza. It will be much safer for her there." She couldn't help but want better things for the pair after what they'd been through.

He nodded in agreement. "You're a good person, Valentina. You have no idea how much having a job can change that young man's life." Ryan took a step closer and she quickly returned to sweeping. As much as she tried to deny it, the man did things to her insides that just couldn't be explained. Her heart raced faster than just a short time ago when she'd thought a killer was about to invade her space.

"It was you who brought him here." She raised her eyes to meet his. "I guess that makes you a good person also." Her cheeks were flushed.

He smiled and seemed to brush the compliment off. "It's my job."

"I think you try to deny it but you go above and beyond what your job is."

"I—" he started but she interrupted.

"No disagreeing with me. Just take the compliment."

"I still insist on paying for the window." He put his hands on his hips.

"How about you take me out to dinner instead?" The offer came out of her mouth before she had a chance to stop it. His eyes widened. "It's okay if you don't want to. I mean, I know you said we shouldn't get involved. It was stupid of me. It just came out. It must have been all the excitement." She bit her lip and swept with gusto.

Ryan smiled and held his hand out to stop her. "I would be honored to take you out to dinner."

Valentina's mouth dropped open. Her brain debated whether this was a good idea or not. "I…uh…really?"

"I know what I said. Sometimes I overthink things. It's just dinner."

Just dinner? "Well, don't put yourself out." Suddenly, dirt and glass were flying farther than they should. *Men! Just when you think you have them figured out, they go and say something stupid.* Ryan Donavan just became the last person she ever wanted to go out with.

"Look, I didn't mean it that way. Dammit, Valentina, why is it whenever I'm around you I say the stupidest things?"

"Oh, so now it's my fault you're an idiot."

She said it as an insult but it made him laugh. "I didn't say I was an idiot, just that I say stupid things sometimes." He took a step closer. "I can't help it. I came over here to ask you out and then, well, you know what happened."

"You came to ask me out?"

"Yes, I did." He took the broom from her hands. "Will you go out to dinner with me, Miss Caponelli?"

Valentina wished she still had the broom to help keep her upright. The man of her dreams just asked her out after she swore she'd never have anything to do with him again. *What to do, what to do?*

"Well, since you asked so nicely. The answer is yes." It would be one of her biggest regrets if she didn't go through with it.

"Great. Now I can get Danny off my back too."

"Excuse me, what?" She narrowed her eyes at him. "Is this some kind of bet that I walked into?"

"A bet? No, no." He placed his patrol hat back on his head. "I was coming over to ask you out, you just asked me out first."

"I didn't ask you out. I said you could take me out instead of paying for the window. Now tell me why that would make, who is it again, Danny, happy?"

He swore under his breath and took a seat in one of the waiting room chairs. "It's been a long day in a long week in a long month. My coworkers think I need to take some time off and, uh, date."

"So you picked me?" Somehow it irked her instead of having a more positive effect.

"It seemed like a good idea at the time."

"Now you're not so sure."

"No. I didn't mean it that way. I've wanted to

119

ask ever since the accident."

Loud boots sounded from the entryway and Dominic's large frame filled the door. "What the hell happened here?" He had a hand on the gun in his side holster but let go when he saw she was safe.

Valentina gave him the abbreviated version of events that led to the broken window.

"It's actually a good thing this happened. They gave us the wrong damn door. We ordered the one with bullet proof glass." Dom made some calls and then addressed Valentina. "I'll take you home, then come back and stay until it gets fixed."

"I'll take her home," Ryan offered.

"It's no trouble, I can wait," Valentina argued. "I'm not a little kid."

"No, but you are the daughter of a Don and the sister of Roman. He'll take you home," Dominic instructed.

"What?" That was the last thing she expected him to say, and she dragged Dom by the arm into her office. "You want me to go with him? What would Roman say?"

"He would trust my opinion, and despite what you think, he trusts Donavan. Tyler told me all the trouble he's been and that the cop never gave up on him. The last thing I need is you sitting here all night watching me fix the damn door. Roman will have someone watching your house all night. I'll pick you up in the morning."

"Okay, okay. I'll get out of your hair." Her shoulders drooped. Her confidence was at an all-time low. Dom couldn't wait to get rid of her and the man of her dreams only asked her out to please his coworkers. She felt like a dupe, and Valentina Caponelli was no one's fool.

Chapter Thirteen

Ryan

It was a quiet drive to her home. He'd made a mess of things, that was for sure. Ryan knew all the right things to say to get a confession from a criminal, but talking to a member of the opposite sex left him feeling less than cool.

When he pulled into her driveway, the woman was out of the car faster than a bank robber fleeing the scene. Unbuckling his seatbelt, he jumped out of the car and followed her up to her door.

"Thanks for the ride but I'm good now." Her hands shook as she fumbled for her keys and they fell to the ground.

"Here, let me help." Ryan bent at the same time as Val and they bumped heads.

"Ouch." They both came up rubbing their foreheads and starring at each other.

Ryan broke the silence first. "This is stupid."

"What?"

"This whole situation." He held out his hand,

palm up. "Give me the keys. Let's go inside and talk."

"Why, is that another bet?" She tossed her keychain into his hand and he unlocked the door.

"There is no bet. Can I come in?"

"Yeah. I guess." It was said without conviction but he'd take it. Val turned on the lights and his eyes automatically lowered to her shapely calves as she wandered over to the living room and took a seat on the couch. The room had similar colors to her office, warm burgundies and dark wood. It suited her and it gave warmth to the room, something that she was not giving him.

He took off his hat. Why didn't he just leave the damn thing in the car? "I'm not good at this stuff, okay? I don't like dating, and if you knew the story of my parents, you'd understand why I haven't gotten involved with anyone for more than one night." Ryan paused to let that sink in but it just seemed to make her more confused. "Like I said, I've always thought you were the most beautiful woman in the world and way out of my league, but I would like to take you out, if you'll have me."

Her lips parted but still she was quiet. He took that as a sign to continue.

"I don't care what your brother thinks and I don't care who your father is or what he's done. I'm interested in you and only you."

This time she bit her lip in a cute but sexy way. Her legs crossed and uncrossed. He could almost hear the gears turning in the smart brain of hers.

"Well, what's your verdict, counselor?" Ryan swallowed as Valentina reached down to slowly remove first one and then the other shoe. Those stupid high heels made him worry that she would break her neck, yet he loved the way they made her legs look. Once the stilettoes were off, she stood up and strolled his way.

"My verdict is," she crossed her arms in front of her chest and studied him from head to toe, "that you have a lot of work to do. At first, I was very excited to go out with you, but now I don't trust you. I need to get that back." Her dark brown eyes shone.

"You know you can trust me." He pointed to his badge.

"All I know is that I've had a school crush on you for way too long," Valentina confessed. "It's time to grow up."

He glanced down at her bare feet "We're not in school anymore."

"No, we're not." She reached behind him and pulled open the door. "Thanks again for driving me home. Good night, Officer Ryan."

He put on his hat but wasn't ready to leave just yet. "I'll see you tomorrow, and I'm not taking no for an answer."

"Good night." This time she gave him a shove, but at least there was a smile on her face.

"Okay, but lock your door behind me." He stepped outside. "And if you hear anything or need anything, just give me a call and I'll be back in a flash."

"That won't be necessary." She pulled the screen door shut.

"I'm serious. Two women have been killed in

less than a week."

The smile died on her lips. "I have a gun and Roman sent me a text that a couple of the guys would be here soon."

"Maybe I'd better wait until they get here." The words had barely left his mouth when a dark SUV pulled up out front. The mob squad was here. It killed him to leave but Valentina would be better protected than just about everyone else in Genoa. She had a private security team courtesy of her brother or father any time she needed it.

The woman was basically mafia royalty, if there was such a thing. A knot started to from in his gut, or maybe it was an ulcer. He was an officer of the law and he was standing on the front porch of the daughter of a crime boss. There was no place in this world that a relationship with her would work out, but he was going to make it come true.

"I guess I'm not needed, then." The words had barely left his mouth before he felt the sweet touch of her lips on his cheek.

"The whole town needs you." Valentina stepped back and her cheeks were pink. "Thanks again for looking out for me."

"I'll still pay for that window," he insisted.

She reached for the door and half stood behind it. "Just prove that your intentions toward me are honorable. That's all I ask. I don't give a darn about the window."

"You've got a deal." Ryan waited until she closed the door and he heard the click of the lock before leaving.

On the way to his car, he stopped at the black

vehicle and knocked on the window to make sure it was really Roman's men. Once the dark window came down, he relaxed when he recognized them. It was a given that they were hired killers, but so far none of this group had done anything to cause any problems. In fact, they seemed to keep things a little quieter. No one wanted to be on the bad side of the Caponellis.

Ryan got in his squad car and started the engine. He should be tired after such a long day, but he was pumped with energy. Having a killer on the loose had him on edge. Thinking about Valentina wouldn't get him any rest either. There was no sense in going home just yet.

Even though he was off duty, he drove around town to check for things that didn't belong. As he turned down one street, his headlights caught the reflection of a slow-moving vehicle. It was Lucky Bauer. He was sixty years old, looked like he was ninety, and had been married eight times. The nickname Lucky could be taken many different ways, but his luck ran out a few years ago when he hit a mailbox and lost his driver's license after too many DUIs.

Ryan pulled along the guy's riding lawnmower and lowered his window. "Lucky, isn't it a little too late to be out and about?"

"What's it to you? I'm not breaking any laws." It had been Ryan's misfortune to be the arresting officer at the mail box incident. The man had blamed him for his loss of driving independence ever since.

"I'm just concerned about someone coming

along, not seeing you, and running you over."

"Well, you'd be the only one," the man mumbled.

"Can I give you lift? It's getting cold out." No one should be out at night driving a lawnmower through town.

"Nah, I've only got a couple more blocks to go."

"All right, Lucky, but I'm going to follow along so people can scc you."

"Do what you want." The man shrugged him off but Ryan could tell he seemed grateful. Despite all the marriages, the guy had no family to speak of. He let him get ahead and pulled over to the side of the street. The car's headlights helped guide the way. Four blocks down, Lucky pulled into his driveway and waved as Ryan drove by.

Everything seemed quiet in this part of town, so he headed toward the strip mall area. All the businesses were closed but light shone through the brown paper covering the windows of a vacant store just past the cluster of shops in the strip mall. He parked in front of the store, looked around the parking lot, and got out of the car.

Peeking through a spot where the paper had fallen back, he spied the shadow of movement coming from a back room. He went over and knocked on the front door. No one answered. He knocked again. "Anyone in there?" he hollered. "Can you open the door, please?" Still nothing. "It's the police. Open up."

Finally, someone shouted that they were coming.

The door opened and the last person he expected to see inside poked her face out.

"Arianne?" Ryan tried to see behind her. "What are you doing here?"

"Uh, it's my new place."

"Place for what? You opening a store?" There was plastic on the floor and a few boxes scattered around.

"I was thinking about opening a fitness center but it's taking a bit longer than expected with the financing and all. I don't have any equipment yet either."

"I hear ya. Banks aren't very eager to give out money these days."

She put one shoulder on the doorframe and pulled the door tight to the other. "No, they aren't."

"Anyway, I saw the light on and thought I would just check and make sure no one was here that shouldn't be."

"I'm flattered that you're looking out for me with that killer on the loose and all, but I assure you, I'm perfectly safe."

"And what do you know about a killer on the loose?"

Her eyes got big. "Everyone knows about it. Crazy stuff. It's all the talk. You can't keep a secret in a small town. Who would do such a thing?"

"That's what we're going to find out." Ryan leaned against the wall and surveyed the parking lot again. A plastic shopping bag skimmed across the blacktop before the wind picked it up and tossed it in a tree. He zipped his coat up a little higher.

"Feels cold enough to snow."

"I'd invite you in but…" She nodded to the back of the store and winked.

"So you're not alone?" Was this a meeting place for her and someone who didn't want to be seen out in public?

"I'm never alone." She wrapped a strand of hair around her finger.

"Well, I just wanted to make sure everything was good here."

"Everything is good. Night, Officer." Arianne shut the door and the lock clicked in place.

Taking a step away from the door, Ryan shivered. He hurried to his car and settled in the seat.

Was everyone hiding behind locked doors just like Arianne? The engine hummed to life and he warmed his hands by the vents. Fall had come too fast and now winter was trying to push its way in. He took one last drive around town. Danny waved as he passed her out on patrol. It was a given that she'd harass him next time she saw him about being on the job twenty-four hours a day.

His drive took him past Valentina's home again. All was dark but it was comforting to see the glow of a cigarette in her bodyguard's vehicle out front. He drove past her office to see if Dominic had finished the window. Her creepy, long-haired handyman was just testing the lock and it appeared to be pretty much done.

Keeping a low profile, Ryan drove the rest of the way down the street. All was quiet except for the antique store Danny and he were going to check out tomorrow. He stopped a block away and turned off his lights. Inside, there was movement, but with all the stuff in the window it had been hard to see. Lack of sleep started to hit and he gave in to a yawn. Ryan leaned forward in the seat when he noticed the lights flick off in the store. Soon, a man exited. He was dressed in all black. He looked both ways down the sidewalk, locked and tested the door, and was clutching a money bag tightly to his chest. His collar up and head bent, the man hurried to a dark van parked across the street.

Damn. Ryan tapped the steering wheel with his fist. It was too far away to read the license plate but it was from out of state. He'd drive by tomorrow and get it. Hopefully, the vehicle would be in the same spot. After the van disappeared down the street, Ryan drove slowly by the store. It was called Bygones, and by God he would be back tomorrow to see what was going on and who that man was.

Chapter Fourteen

Despite everything going on, Ryan fell asleep as soon as his head hit the pillow. Danny had worked the night shift, so after changing into street clothes she made her way to the antique store the minute it opened. Her thoughts on the visit were that the guy was friendly enough but certainly didn't go out of his way to help a customer. She said there were some very high-end antiquities in the shop but the rest were reproductions.

As Ryan drove by the van, which was parked in the same spot as the night before, he made a mental note of its plates and called them in as soon as he parked. Ryan spied a flower shop and made a detour to that store. The scent of roses hit him as soon as he entered.

"Can I help you, sir?" a friendly voice called out. She had green tape in one hand and some flowers in the other.

"Yes, are you the owner?" Her nametag said Ivy. He wondered if all of the employees were named after flowers.

Her face went white when she noticed the uniform. "Yes, is there a problem?" Everyone seemed to get nervous when cops were around. Ryan had once stopped someone for going through a traffic light and the guy had peed himself.

"No, nothing to worry about. I was just wondering if I could ask you a couple questions."

"Sure." She set the tape and flowers on the corner and wiped her hands on the apron she was wearing.

"Do you know who owns the antique store next door?" He gestured to her left wall.

"Personally? No. I've seen the guy come in in the morning but he rarely leaves before I do in the evening."

"Never talked to him or even said hi?" He took out a notebook and pen to jot down anything important.

"When he first opened, I stopped over with a welcome plant. He thanked me but that was about it."

"Do you know his name?"

Her face scrunched up. "Uh, Bob. No, wait. Rob. Edward." She snapped her fingers. "Edward something or other."

"Do you know where he's from?"

Ivy put a hand on her hip. "Is he in trouble? Is this something I need to worry about?"

"No, just following up on something. No need to worry."

"I heard about those murders. It's frightening. I bought a gun." The Aerosmith song "Janie's Got a Gun" suddenly played in his head, only it was

132

replaced with *Ivy's Got a Gun*. It was hard to picture the petite flower girl toting a pistol, but he knew from talking to one of the guys at the gun shop that women were becoming his best customers.

"Yes, we are following up on all the leads but it is best to not be alone in the shop, and be sure to keep your doors locked at home and when you are closed here."

"We do that already. Rose is in the back finishing up a bouquet." Looked like he was right about the employees' names. "So, do we need to be concerned about the guy next door?" she asked again.

"Not that we are aware of. Now, do you know where he's from?"

"No." She clicked her fingers. "He does have a Southern accent. Does that help?"

He jotted down *Rhett Butler voice*. "Thanks, you've been very helpful, Ivy."

"Anytime."

He turned to leave.

"Hey, Officer. We have roses on sale today. Can we send something to a lady friend of yours?"

Ten minutes and fifty dollars later, Ryan left the flower shop and entered Bygones. A brass bell above the door announced his arrival.

Who appeared to be the same man in black as last night glanced up from some books on his counter and then quickly returned to studying them.

"Morning," Ryan said as he approached the man. "Are you the owner?"

The guy was about his height, had salt and

pepper hair, and a pair of reading glasses on the end of his nose. He looked to be in his late forties. "Yes, can I help you?" He pinched the glasses between the lenses and placed them on the counter.

"Do you have any old-fashioned flour sack towels? You know, the ones with the days of the week on them?"

"Yes, follow me." Ryan noticed a business card by the cash register. He read the name Edward Davis and stuffed one in his pocket.

"Is this you on the card? Are you Edward?"

"Yes, this is my shop," the man said over his shoulder.

Ryan trailed him through the packed store. There were a lot of shelves stacked with knickknacks, books, and some other things that he had no idea what they were.

"Here they are. These are vintage but we also sell reproductions."

Ryan felt the material of both—the new ones were stiff while the vintage towels were silky and a brighter white. "Do you sell a lot of these?"

"You don't seem like the type of guy who appreciates embroidery."

"No, can't say as I am, but I'm following up on something pertaining to a case."

The man shrugged his shoulders and leaned against a shelf. "I just had a woman leave the store who asked for these also. Is there something going on that I don't know about? Maybe I should raise the price." He scratched his forehead.

"Have you sold any lately?"

"I gave a bunch away when I first opened. It was

a gift with purchase kind of thing. I also have an online store."

"You do?" That opened a whole other option for acquiring the towels. They didn't have the man power to check every store or auction house on the internet.

"Yes, I have a few things on there. Mostly the new stuff and my more expensive items."

"And what items might those be?"

The man stood up straight and crossed his arms in front of this chest. "Is there a problem, Officer? I get the feeling that you aren't here to shop."

"I'm not. We recently found a towel like this at the scene of a crime and we're trying to locate where it came from."

Edward's face went white. "What kind of crime?"

"I'm not at liberty to say right now." The room got quiet and he figured the helpfulness of Edward Davis was about to run out. People were usually pretty open about answering things to a man in uniform, but once they got a whiff of something more serious, the conversations start to come to an end.

"This doesn't have to do with those murders, does it?" Now he fidgeted with the zipper on his fleece pullover.

"I'm not at—" Ryan started.

"I know, I know. Not at liberty to say. I moved to this town because I thought it was a safe place to live, and now women are being killed right and left. Why aren't you out trying to catch this guy?"

"I'm here following up on a lead."

"Well, you came to the wrong place because I had nothing to do with them."

"I never said you did. Just trying to see who might have purchased any of these items." He motioned toward the shelf full of linens. "How about sad irons? Anyone buy one of them lately?"

"Let me find out." Ryan followed him to his back office, where Edward checked his computer. "Yes, one last week. I remember her. Nice girl named Amy something or other."

"Did you see her any time after that purchase?"

"No." The man's mouth dropped open. "Don't tell me she was one of the girls killed."

"Why would you think that?" It was a simple question, but the response wasn't.

"I don't like your tone. I think you'd better leave now, Officer..." Edward glanced at his name tag.

"Donavan. I was just asking." Ryan studied the man's body language. His face was red and his hands twitched. "I didn't mean to insinuate anything."

"I'm sorry, Officer Donavan. I meant no disrespect but I've recently had a loss as well." That still didn't explain why he thought Amy had been a victim.

"Here's my card if you think of anything else related to those towels or the sad iron."

Reluctantly, the man took his card and tucked it in his pants pocket. The man's whole demeanor had changed and he shook like a leaf.

"I'll show you to the door." Edward took off down the aisle, leaving Ryan no option but to follow. Along the way, Ryan searched for anything that appeared out of place. Not that he would know what was out of place in a place like this. The price tag on some elaborate furniture near the door did catch his eye though.

He whistled. "Wow, that's some fancy stuff." There was a bed with elaborate carvings and a dresser that was equally as nice.

"It's pre-Civil War era and in exceptional shape. I'm sure it's above your pay range." Edward opened the door.

That was rude. "Do you have some kind of problem with cops? I'm sensing some hostility here." Ryan stood in the doorway but was not about to leave.

"Not at all. Like I said, I've recently had a loss. These murders are bringing up bad memories."

"I'm sorry for your loss." He took a step down and backward out the door. The man was still a few inches shorter than him. "Before I leave, what size shoe do you wear?"

"Ten." Edward slammed the door in his face.

After a quick stop at the Java Shop, he was back at the station pouring over the case files. One of those day of the week towels had been found at Tracy's, along with a bag from Bygones. It wasn't until he noticed Edward's shoes that he remembered a footprint in the mud behind the house of the first murder. A photo of it was in the file. That could be anything, but it didn't hurt to keep track of people who wore size ten shoes. So far, Edward Davis was at the top of that list of suspects. There was something not right about that guy. Aside from the print, nothing was out of place at either scene except for the towels.

The autopsies revealed they'd both been injected in the neck with a drug. They were still waiting for the toxicology report to find out what that drug or drugs were. It was just getting odder and odder. All things pointed to this being a possible serial killer. It appeared that Tracy had hit her head when she fell, but she was ultimately smothered to death. Amy must have seen the needle coming and struggled. It was the iron to the head that was her ultimate demise. Both cases hit him in the heart and the stomach. Their parents were devastated.

He studied the info from the license plate. It belonged to Davis. According to the record, his previous address was in Georgia. That explained the accent. After a more thorough search of the internet, it was revealed that the man's wife was dead. He found an obituary for Elizabeth LaGrander-Davis. Apparently, Edward had married well. His wife came from a very wealthy Southern family. There was no mention of how the woman died.

After a few more hours, he still had no answers but his cop radar was on high alert. Elizabeth had only been in her late forties, yet there was no mention of illness, car accident, or anything really. According to all accounts, Edward had been the sole benefactor of her large estate. Ryan's cell phone vibrated and he glanced at the screen. It was just a text from the local gas station for a discount on gas but it reminded him to listen again to the message Danny had sent earlier.

"Hi, Ry. That guy was odd. Seemed surprised anyone would be interested in the towels yet he has a lot of them. He inherited all the merchandise from his wife. She had a shop and the furniture was hers also. That's some high-end shit. Chippendale's quality, and I'm not talking the dancers. We might want to check and see what happened to the wife. I'm hitting the hay. Be glad to be back on the day shift tomorrow. Text me what you found out. Thanks."

Taking a risk, Ryan looked up the number for the nearest police station to where the Davis couple last lived. He hit the number and crossed his fingers.

"McGraw County Police. How may I direct your call?" The person on the phone sounded like a native to the area.

"This is Officer Ryan Donavan calling from the Lake Genoa Police Department in Wisconsin. I was hoping to talk to someone there who may have known Elizabeth LaGrander-Davis."

Silence.

"Hello?" Ryan hoped he'd not been hung up on.

"Uh, yes. What did you say, Officer Ryan?"

"I'm hoping to find out more about how Elizabeth LaGrander-Davis died and see how it might relate to a case we have here." It was a risk suggesting it but maybe he'd get lucky.

"Please hold."

He waited and waited until a gruff voice finally said, "Hello, this is Officer Moore. You're asking about Mrs. LaGrander-Davis?"

After giving his credentials again in a deep, authoritative voice, Ryan continued his story. "We have an ongoing murder investigation here that I think might be similar to her case."

"Go on." At least the man was listening.

It was a gamble but Ryan wasn't giving up. "We've had two young women murdered here in the last couple weeks. They were injected with a sedative and then killed."

There was no sound on the other end of the phone until the man finally answered. "Unfortunately, that isn't too uncommon in this day and age. What does that have to do with Elizabeth?"

"We found items from an antique store owned by her husband at each location."

"Damn." The voice on the phone cursed.

"You want to tell me about it?" Ryan's heart rate jacked up.

Officer Moore exhaled. "I'll tell you what I know, but you didn't hear it from me. Okay?"

"Deal." Ryan grabbed a pen and some paper.

"That's exactly how we found Elizabeth LaGrander-Davis and several other women in the area. She was from a very wealthy and powerful family around here. They didn't want her tied up in all of this. Paid a big city attorney to keep everything about her death under wraps."

"Was there anything found at the scenes? Something the victims all had in common?" He tapped his pen on the desk.

"Yes, it's the one thing we kept out of the papers. We found an embroidered towel with each body. A day of the week kind of thing. Monday is wash day, Tuesday is mending, and on and on."

Shit. Ryan ran his fingers through his hair. This sick individual hadn't just killed twice but many times.

"What about Elizabeth's husband? I don't have to tell you that the husband is usually the one who did it in most cases."

"Of course. Her parents hated the guy. Thought he was the killer but we had no evidence. The man was out of town during the time we found one of the victims. It just didn't make sense."

"What didn't?" Besides the whole damn thing. Ryan mulled all the details over in his head for the fiftieth time.

"It's as if the women weren't afraid of the person who did this. That it was someone they all knew and trusted. They let the person inside their homes and there was rarely a struggle."

It was the same in Tracy's case.

"So whatever happened to the husband?" *And why did he show up here?* Ryan wanted to ask.

"Elizabeth's parents didn't want to see him again. Said it was like a kick in the face to see him out and about while their daughter was dead and buried. He always claimed his innocence and I think he really did care for his wife. Elizabeth wasn't the saint they thought she was."

"How so?" It was like a soap opera playing out in real life.

"Elizabeth liked to sleep around." Moore spoke in a hushed tone.

"And you know this for sure?"

"As sure as I know she had a heart-shaped birthmark on her right hip." In other words, the officer knew Mrs. LaGrander up close and personal.

"So you knew her quite well, then?" Ryan jotted a few notes down.

"As did a few others that I know. Like I said, she wasn't as innocent as her parents thought or wanted to believe."

"So, again, what happened to the husband?" Ryan tried to get Moore back on track.

"The LaGranders had a place somewhere up in Wisconsin. They gave him the property if he promised to get the hell out of town. As far as I know, he took them up on the offer."

"It looks like he did, as the man lives here now."

"Shit. And now the same thing is happening there? Guy might not be as innocent as we thought." Moore exhaled loudly.

"No one ever is. Well, thanks, Officer Moore. Could you send us all the info you have from those cases? I think the person who may have killed the women there, whether it's Mrs. LaGrander-Davis's husband or not, just came to our town."

Chapter Fifteen

Valentina

As much as she tried to distract herself from thoughts of Officer Ryan, it was a losing battle. Every time the phone rang or someone came in her office, she bounced out of her chair like her name had been called on a game show. Whenever she pictured him in his uniform, she just about swooned.

The sweet scent of roses drifted her way. He'd sent flowers. She did a little happy dance in her chair. It was a start, but they still had a long, long way to go. The clock on the wall said it was time to close her doors. Tyler was back in school but had come by afterward to help with some yard work and filing papers.

Just like yesterday, she'd promise to stay inside until Dominic returned. Her finger hovered over her phone to call and thank Ryan for the gift but she remained strong. He needed to come to her.

The phone buzzed. She jumped and dropped it in

her lap. It was Ryan.

Trying to remain calm, Val took a deep breath and answered.

"Are you almost done for the day?" His voice made her stomach flutter.

"Yes, all locked up and wanting for Dom to come back from dropping off Tyler."

"How's the kid doing?" Ryan asked.

"He's good. He sure admires you."

Laughter filled the air. "The kid hates me, what are you talking about?"

"He really doesn't. You know how boys that age try to act tough. He knows that you are looking out for him."

"Well, someone has to. It's hard growing up without a dad."

"You are a good role model for him. Who knows, maybe he will go into law enforcement."

"Now I know you're pulling my leg. Although that is what my uncle encouraged me to do after the death of my father."

There was a lull before she remembered the bouquet on the table in front of the window. "Thank you for the flowers. They're lovely."

"I was at the flower shop. There was a sale, so I thought, why not?" He was rambling.

"You made that sound so unromantic," she teased.

"Sorry. Like I said, I'm not good at this stuff. You're the first person I've ever sent flowers to." That thought touched her more than the gift.

She rose, smoothed her skirt, and strolled over to touch the petals of one of the flowers. It was soft between her thumb and index finger. "So what did I do to deserve such an honor?"

Her finger stilled as she wanted for his response.

"I've been a loner all my life, but I don't want to be anymore. Seeing those young girls dead just confirmed that fact." Her admiration rose with the realization of how much he cared about others.

Ryan continued, "When I saw the flowers, you were the first person I thought of. I've never had that happen before."

"What do you think that means?" She placed a hand on her hip and hoped.

"I think it means that I don't want to just admire you from a distance. I didn't ask you out on a dare. I really wanted to."

A big smile crossed her face. "Keep going." She giggled, suddenly feeling like a school girl instead of a twenty-something attorney at law.

"So, what are you doing tomorrow?"

"I think I'm going out with you." And she wasn't taking no for an answer.

He said to dress casually but that wasn't something that she did well. The outfit from the western dance didn't seem right either. She finally settled for a pair of slim fitting pants, boots, and a sweater. There was a chill in the air but it was still a beautiful fall day. Not that it was any of his business, but she sent a text to her brother asking that he call her guard dogs off for the day. The last thing she needed was a bunch of guys in suits following them around.

Her phone buzzed. It was Roman. "Does he have a gun on him?"

"He's a cop, I would assume so."

"I don't assume anything. Find out and I'll call them off."

She stomped her foot and marched over to the door. The SUV was still out there. Her heart leapt when she spied Ryan's truck heading down her street. He parked in her driveway, waved at her bodyguards, and hopped up her front stairs two at a time.

Valentina opened the door as he stuck a hand out, ready to hit the doorbell.

"Uh, hi." His smile took her breath away, but first things first.

"Do you have a gun on you?"

Ryan moved his jean jacket to the side. "Yes, why?" There was a pistol holstered to his side and she snapped a pic with her phone.

Her fingers flew across her phone's keyboard and then she focused on the vehicle at the end of her sidewalk. Thirty seconds later, it started and drove off down the street. Val dragged Ryan in the house by the arm of his coat.

"What was that all about?"

"I had to promise Roman that you had a gun on you before he would release the hounds from watching me."

"Interesting prerequisite for dating one's sister." It would take some getting used to but it was a challenge he was ready to accept.

"Well, everyone's on edge with that killer still on the loose. Any leads yet?" She grabbed her keys and stuffed her phone in her purse. "It's been all over the news. I can't imagine what those women must have gone through." Valentina shivered.

"I can't say much at this time but we do have some leads that we are following up on and a couple people we are keeping a close eye on. I can't say I blame Roman for wanting to keep you safe. I know if I had a sister, I wouldn't let her out of my sight either."

The mention of his lack of family broke her heart. "Well, let's try and not think about it for now. I'm looking forward to whatever it is that we are doing today."

"Do you have a preference?" He raised an eyebrow.

"No, surprise me." She felt giddy.

"Prepare to be surprised." He placed his hand on the lower part of her back and guided her out the door and to his truck. As soon as she was inside and he joined her, the musky scent of his aftershave warmed her from the inside out. It was not overpowering but just enough to encourage one closer, and oh, how she wanted to be closer.

The inside of the cab also smelled like dog. "You have a dog?"

"No, it's the K-9 officer."

"You call your dog an officer?"

"Milo is a member of the police department. He usually stays with one of the other officers but I take him every once in a while."

"So, your no relationship rule applies to pets

too?"

"I would like one, I'm just not home enough to take care of one." The truck roared to life. "I'm kind of married to the job right now. I can't stand the fact that the town is on edge."

There were dark shadows under his eyes, making it obvious he'd been going on little sleep. A twinge of guilt flickered when she thought about how she had men keeping her safe when she slept at night while others didn't have that luxury. "I know Roman has had some of his tech guys searching the web for anything similar to these cases."

He turned her way in the seat. "Really?"

"Now don't be upset. He's just trying to help."

He placed his hand on hers and looked directly in her eyes. "I'm not upset in the least. If he finds anything, anything at all, please let me know."

"I will." She sent her brother another text. "Now let's talk about more pleasant topics. Where are you taking me today?"

"I noticed you had a few pictures of the water and lighthouses hanging in your office so I thought you might like a boat ride and to visit the closest thing we have to one."

"I've always been fascinated by lighthouses, but where are we going to find one here?" In no time at all they were pulling into the parking lot at the docks. The lake was huge with a walking path that went all the way around, including in front of Roman's lakeside estate. The docks had a huge yacht club that held wedding receptions and was the starting place for the local boat tours. It had been built back in the 1930s as a work program during the Depression.

"Shall we?" Ryan got out of the truck.

The sun shone off the water and it sparkled like diamonds. So transfixed was she with the sight that she didn't realize he had opened and was standing by her door.

"I haven't been this excited since I don't know when." They walked along the sidewalk, shaded by a tree here and there. Despite the early hour, there were joggers, families strolling with kids, and couples of all ages out for a walk.

"You don't get out much, do you?" he joked.

"No, I don't. All work and no play, so to speak."

"I guess we have more in common than you think." He took her hand to led the way and a jolt of electricity shot up her arm.

"I can't remember the last time I was on a boat ride. I went on a Mediterranean cruise with the family when I was in high school, but nothing like this."

"Well, I can't afford a fancy cruise like that, but hopefully you will like this."

It never occurred to her that money might be an issue between them with all the other things that were already there, but she was going to nip this one in the bud right away. She stopped and looked him square in the face. "It isn't money or expensive things that impress me. It's character, honestly, and loyalty."

"Then we will get along just fine." He squeezed her hand.

Ryan paid for their tickets while she admired the boats. He'd admitted to never having been on one of these tours before. There were cruise boats of all kinds depending on the tour. Some were very big for large parties, while others were smaller. The lake was famous for its wood boats and several were bobbing with the waves.

"Are you ready?" He waved the tickets in the air.

"Yes." She tucked her hand in the crook of his elbow and let him lead the way to their tour boat. It was a small open one, as Ryan had selected a specialized tour. In Chicago, she was never allowed to be out in the open like this—what if one of her father's enemies spied her and tried to take her out?

Fortunately, things had calmed down in the last few years. The turf wars were over and no one seemed to care about the Caponellis in Lake Genoa. This was their territory now. She took a deep breath to inhale the fresh air and the freedom of being just a normal couple out for a ride. The sunlight felt wonderful on her face, but once the boat left the dock, she shivered. Ryan took off his coat and wrapped it around her shoulders. It was warm from his body heat and instantly took the chill off. Valentina snugged closer and enjoyed being out with him.

The tour guide narrated the history of the lake and the many mansions that lined it. The boat didn't go as far as Roman's estate, but if it had, she wondered what they would have said about the place. Notorious mob heir or local business man?

It was an easy conversation that they fell into as they pointed at different points of interest along the way. Soon, the boat docked on the other side of the lake.

"Why are we stopping here?"

"I couldn't find a lighthouse, but this is the closest thing we have here." He interlocked his fingers with hers and led her off the boat. "I hope you don't mind stairs. There are only one hundred and twenty of them."

"Yikes. I might need mouth to mouth by the time I get to the top."

"You're in luck. I'm an expert at that," he teased.

She glanced up to see a beautiful old estate with a tower for overlooking the lake. It was breathtaking. Staring at the many steps, she thought she just might have to test Ryan's offer.

Chapter Sixteen

For the next hour and a half they took the guided tour of the Black Pointe Estate. It was a huge home built back in 1888. The tour of the first and second floors was fascinating considering everything had arrived there by boat and then had been carried up all those stairs.

Its gardens were still blooming and even more exquisite now that the leaves of the surrounding trees were just as colorful as the flowers. There were shades of gold, rust, and orange shimmering everywhere. A bubbling fountain enticed her away from the other tourists.

"It's like our own private garden." She twirled around and stopped to smell the mums. "It's so beautiful."

Valentina rose and turned around. Ryan stood in front of her a look of wonder on his face. "Not as beautiful as what's standing in front of me.'"

"Oh yeah?" She was lightheaded. Whether it was from getting up so fast or the man in front of was yet to be decided.

His hand cupped her cheek and his thumb caressed her lip. "Unless you speak up, I'm going to kiss you, Valentina Caponelli." He paused and she said nothing.

It felt like the world was spinning too fast when his lips touched hers. Ryan wrapped one hand around her waist while the other gently caressed her cheek. It was a sweet first kiss after the one they'd shared in the parking lot not too long ago, but it still knocked her socks off. The more he kissed her, the more her thoughts drifted from wholesome to sensual.

He may not have believed in relationships, but the man definitely knew how to kiss. Valentina moaned and pressed closer. Ryan stopped. His eyelids were heavy and there was a grin on his face. "You do that again and I might drag you into the bushes."

"You keep kissing me like that and I'll go willingly." Her cheeks were flushed, and it wasn't the sun that made her skin heat up.

"Everyone ready? It's time to get on board," the tour guide hollered from the porch of the estate.

"It's time to go, I guess." Val turned to leave but Ryan pulled her back.

"One last kiss." He gave her a quick peck on the lips. "I will always think of this place and remember this time." It was a sweet and sentimental statement from an all business, loner kind of guy. Her mouth opened but nothing came out.

"What's this?" he joked as they walked hand in hand toward the rest of the travelers. "I've never seen an attorney with nothing to say."

"I guess I never expected to see this side of you."

"What side?"

"Don't take this the wrong way."

"This doesn't sound good." He placed a hand on his chest.

"It is good. I know you're a good man despite the tough guy, take no prisoners attitude. It's the same with my brother. No one knows the people he helps because he knows how much he really cares will make him look weak. You're the same way."

They stopped walking and Valentina continued. "What you do helping Tyler, you didn't have to do that. I know you have been spending more hours than you are probably being paid for to help hunt down the Housewife Killer." The local news channel started calling the murderer that after finding out about the towels at both crime scenes. "I'm glad you are letting your guard down and showing me the real you."

Ryan shifted from foot to foot. "We'd better go or we'll miss the boat."

"I think we have time for one more." She leaned in and kissed him. The grin he gave her when she was done took her breath away. His mouth to mouth training may have come in handy at some point the way things were going. Valentina felt joy like she hadn't in a long time. She grabbed his hand and they hurried down the stairs. They were the last two aboard and the captain teased that they should get a room.

On the return trip, they sat a lot closer than the first time and held hands. When they got off the boat it was time for lunch and they ate at one of the beachside restaurants. It featured some memorabilia from the Playboy club that use to be there. As they passed a display featuring an old red bunny costume, Ryan stopped and pointed. "You'd look good in that."

She swatted his arm. "One kiss and you're telling me how to dress." She studied the outfit. It was quite revealing, but she did look good in red.

"I think we've had more than one so far, and I didn't say you had to dress that way, just that it would look good on you." He led her to a table just off the beach. "I wouldn't mind seeing you in a bunny outfit." Ryan winked and held out her chair for her to take a seat.

They both dined on bacon cheese burgers made with local cheese, deep fried cheese curds, and french fries. "I love cheese." Valentina bit into a gooey deep-fried curd. Steam rolled off the half still in her hand.

"Welcome to Wisconsin." Ryan dipped some fries in ranch dressing.

"Do you ever think you'll go back to Chicago?" she wondered.

"To live?"

"Yes." Genoa was where she wanted to stay. It already felt like home.

"No, this is home now."

"Roman loves it here. He can't wait to start a family. I think I will like it here too." She took a drink of the best lemonade she'd ever had.

"You've got two businesses here now. That will keep you busy."

She wiped her mouth with a napkin and set it by

her plate. "I really haven't done much with Firenza. I feel bad about that. I begged Roman to buy it for me yet he's been paying Madison and others to manage it while I finished school."

"I'm sure he's turning a hefty profit. Roman doesn't seem like the kind of man who loses money doing anything."

"Yeah, I guess." She shrugged. "I just feel like I should be doing more."

"If he needed your help, I'm sure he'd ask. Didn't you get Tyler's mom a job there?"

"Yes, she's learning fast and doing great."

"Well, looks like you did a good thing for your business and someone else."

"Yeah, I guess so." She picked up her burger again. "That's why I became a lawyer. My father may have insisted I become one so I could help the family, but I really want to help everyone."

"Don't worry about what others think. You do what you want to do."

"Did you always want to be a cop?" It interested her how people ended up in the careers they chose.

"No. I was in a shit load of trouble after my parents died." He stretched back in his chair and tossed the napkin on the table. "My uncle got me on the straight and narrow."

It was on the tip of her tongue to ask about his parents. She really hadn't thought about it in years. Until she decided that she wanted to pursue a relationship with him, that is.

"Can I get you any dessert?" The waitress had returned to clear their plates.

Ryan leaned forward and rested his elbows on

his knees. "Want anything?"

She was stuffed and shook her head.

"Just the check, please."

"Here, let me get it." Valentina reached for her purse. "You paid for the tour."

"Nope. Today is my treat." He handed his card to the waitress.

"Well, next time is mine." Oh, how she wanted a next time. "I could cook us some dinner."

Ryan looked agreeable and then stilled.

She placed a hand on his. "Don't worry. It's only coffee that I suck at."

"I'm sure I'll love whatever you make, plus it gets me a second date."

"You think so, huh?"

The waitress returned and he quickly signed and took care of the bill. "Yeah. Where to next?" He stood and pulled her chair out.

They walked back toward the center of town and into some of the shops. Clearly, Ryan wasn't as excited as she was about shopping but he was a good sport. The only store he refused to go in was the new antique shop called Bygones. When she pressed him for more, he finally said it involved a case so he didn't want to scare away any suspects.

She took him at his word and they skipped that one. They stopped at a gun store and it was the first one that he seemed really enthusiastic about. Valentina impressed him with her knowledge of handguns. Growing up in a mafia family, she had to be aware of the dangers all around her. Even now she had her gun with her. Roman had known that but wanted more protection for her.

They had a late dinner but still didn't want the evening to end. "How about going to a speakeasy?"

"A what?" Valentina's ears perked up. She loved everything 1920s.

"There's a place up a block that has a speakeasy in the basement."

"I'm game."

"Let's go. I'll find the password." She followed his fingers on the phone as he found the Facebook page that listed the password for the night. "Found it." He showed her the screen.

The place was a beautiful 1850s mansion. The back carriage house that used to be the home for the horses had been redone into elaborate guest rooms. There were even a couple rooms in the house that came with butler service.

They found the door to the speakeasy and knocked. A small panel at eye level slid open and a man in a fedora peered out. "Password."

"I love Valentina," Ryan answered.

Did she hear him right?

"Wrong." Fedora hat man frowned.

Ryan shook his head. "I mean, I love Valentino."

The slider shut and the door opened. Jazz music flowed out and they eagerly stepped into the dimly lit area. There were people sitting around the 1920s themed bar. Some of them were in costumes, including the bartenders who sported suspenders and garters on their arms.

"I love the flapper dresses," Valentina squealed as she saw a girl dance by in one.

"You'd look good in that," Ryan whispered in her ear.

"You thought I'd look good in a bunny outfit also." She poked him in the side.

"Valentina, you're so beautiful. You could wear a garbage bag and look good."

"You're so sweet. I thought you said you weren't good at relationships." She reached for his hand and held it. "You are making great waves with me."

"I guess I just never found someone I was willing to pursue until now." His gaze dropped to her lips and then back to her eyes.

"Evening, what can I get you two lovebirds?" a waitress interrupted.

"Whatever the special is, we'll have two." He quickly sent the young woman on her way.

"And you want to pursue me?" Could she hope?

"Yes. Do you want to pursue me?" Ryan tapped his finger on her hand.

"Here you go." The waitress arrived at the wrong moment and placed their drinks on the table. They were pink and fruity.

Valentina took a sip and pondered what to say next. Should she bare her soul to him?

"Well?" He didn't touch his drink, instead resting his elbows on the table.

She didn't want to come across as some kind of stalker who had always admired him from afar. Valentina hung out with several girls in her brother's class and they all thought the new student was a hottie. Ryan had transferred as a sophomore and had kept to himself for the most part. He never attended any dances or after school activities except for sports. Racking her brain, there were no girlfriends of his that she could think of.

159

She rolled her eyes before meeting his. "Well, if you must know, I have always thought of you as very handsome."

"That's all?" He finally took a drink and then frowned at the girly drink.

"Isn't that enough?"

He shifted in his seat. "Well, I just thought I remembered seeing you a few times at school games and I see you liked the department Facebook page some time ago."

"I'm supporting local law enforcement. Is that a crime? And my brother was on the same team," she teased.

"I guess I was just hoping you had noticed me." He shook his head and rubbed his jaw. "Shit, I have an easier time talking to criminals."

It touched her heart that this brave man was showing her his vulnerable side. He was trying to gain her trust and be sincere.

"I think you are doing just fine."

"I'm sorry for being a jerk. I've been fighting my attraction for you for so long." He leaned back in his chair. "I didn't want to wait anymore, especially now that you work in my field."

"What do you mean?"

"You see car accidents and such." He stilled. It was obvious that the recent deaths were still affecting him. "Life is too short to never experience love."

"You've never been in love?" Valentina crossed and then uncrossed her ankles.

"No, have you?" He motioned for the waitress and ordered a beer, pushing his drink toward her.

"Well..." She resisted the urge to say she'd loved him from afar. "No, I guess not. I've rarely had time to date. Just knowing who my father is has been enough to scare off most guys."

"I don't care who your family is and I don't scare easy." Ryan took her hand in his.

"You really don't care that I'm from a mafia family?"

"Nope. Does it bother you that I'm a cop?"

"No." Her heart soared. The place was packed and noisy, yet all that mattered was that they were there together and he only had eyes for her.

The rest of the evening flew by. The conversation stayed mostly to present day. Ryan was a diehard Packers fan while Valentina decided to stay loyal to the Bears. They tried a few of the jazz dances but both had two left feet. They were mostly just content to sit in silence and enjoy each other's company. It was nice to escape the bad stuff happening, even if it was only for a few hours.

Chapter Seventeen

Ryan had to work on Sunday so Valentina stayed home to get things unpacked and put away. That didn't take very long. Her life had been so busy with school that there hadn't been time to accumulate much stuff. Her family home had everything anyway. Valentina never realized before how much she never lacked for anything in the way of home comforts. Roman's house was full of everything a person could ever need, including a home gym, pool, and home theatre.

If she was with Ryan, time together mattered more than material things. With him, she'd have a chance at something she never dreamed would happen. Having someone to love. Someone to start a life with. Maybe even start a family with. Valentina wanted a love like Roman and Madison's. It was too early to think it could be but there was hope.

It had only been the first date, but if Ryan would have wanted to the spend the night, it would have been hard to say no. Being a gentleman, he texted her brother to have her bodyguards waiting for them when they returned. Even with her security system Ryan still insisted on checking out the house to make sure there was no one hiding under the bed or in the closets. Then he'd given her another earth shattering kiss good night. A pool of heat hit her lower belly just thinking about it.

Now that the house was in order, she enjoyed some coffee that Dom had dropped off after replacing the guys who had spent the night keeping watch on her place. They were both now in the living room watching the news. The deaths of the two women had been publicly declared murders and the police were looking for any clues to link them. There was a special hotline set up for people to call in any tips they may have had. It was warm in her house but she shivered. Who would kill them and for what reason?

The only information given by the police was that the deaths had involved some kind of head trauma. Used to being so busy, having nothing to do made her restless.

"What do you think really happened?" Her heart ached thinking of the victims' families.

Never one for many words, Dominic just grunted.

"Dom, I'm going out." She grabbed a down vest from the closet. He got up and went to the door.

"Where to?" His hand was on the doorknob.

"I don't know. I just can't sit here anymore." She trailed him out the door and down the sidewalk. "A walk. Anything."

They headed down the street to where the shops

were. It wasn't her intended stop but she didn't feel like strolling around the lake. Not all the shops were open. The tourist season had ended so only a few businesses still had the open sign lit up out front.

The one Ryan refused to take her to, Bygones, had its lights on. "Let's stop at that one."

"Since when do you like old shit?" Dominic didn't seem happy about accompanying her to the shops. He tended to scare the other customers when they went in places.

"I don't, but it's open. You can stay out here if you like," she suggested.

"Your brother would have my nuts if I let you out of my sight." He reached for the door.

"Thanks for the disturbing visual." A bell above the entrance jingled as they walked inside.

It was at least a minute or two before a man came from the back. "Can I help you?"

"Are you the owner?" Valentina asked after she shooed Dom over to look at some antique swords.

"Yes. Is there something I can help you with?" He flashed her a big smile and placed both hands on the counter.

"No, I just wanted to introduce myself." She reached out her hand and he shook it. "I'm Valentina Caponelli. I'm an attorney and just opened my office about a block away. I saw you were also new so thought I would just stop in and say hi."

"Well, hopefully, I will never have a need for a lawyer but I'm glad you stopped by. It's a pleasure to meet you, Mrs. Caponelli."

"It's miss," she corrected him.

"My mistake, I figured someone as beautiful as you would already be taken."

That statement brought Dominic back to her side and the smile on Edward's face disappeared.

"I am taken." Well, even if she wasn't, that was her story. "But thanks for the compliment."

Edward swallowed as his gaze drifted to the man by her side.

"Ah, this is a friend of mine, Dominic Scarlatti."

The antique owner just nodded and neither held out their hands.

"So," Edward said after a moment, "is there anything I can get for you or show you?"

Both were shocked when Dom spoke. "Yes, the knife in the case."

An hour and a few hundred bucks later, they left Bygones. Valentina found a Tiffany lamp she liked for her office and Dom purchased a vintage dagger. The two men actually had a civil conversation about knives, swords, and other deadly weapons that left her feeling a bit queasy. Although Edward was polite and didn't do anything threatening, she wouldn't want to be alone with the guy. He just gave off a bad vibe, maybe a sense of sadness.

As soon as they arrived home, Roman called. "I need your help." Finally, she would have something to do. "Can you come over?"

"Sure, we're leaving now." Dominic drove her to her brother's house, where they found him in his office.

"What's up, Romeo?" The glare he gave her would have most men pissing themselves, but she knew he'd never hurt her.

"I'm going over the files from the housewife murders." He stretched and leaned back in his chair. His desk was littered with papers.

"How did you get these?" She paled when some of the photos of the victims came into focus. "Who could do such a thing?"

"I've seen worse." Dominic picked up a photo. "But even I would never do that to a woman. Maybe it was a woman who did this."

Valentina ignored him. "Again, how do you have these? These are confidential files from the police department. See, on the front it says *Confidential, Property of the Lake Genoa Police Department.*" She tapped it with her fingers.

"I had our tech guy hack in. I want this monster caught just as bad as the next guy. I thought we could go over this stuff and see if we can find something they missed." Roman studied the photos again. "Do you recognize this work?" Some killers had a signature, especially the hired ones. He held up a photo of Amy and handed it to Dom.

"No, it looks personal, not professional. Could be a lover's quarrel or someone in the wrong place at the wrong time." Dominic picked up the photo of Tracy and shook his head. "Not a mob hit. I'm certain of it."

"Are the girls connected somehow?" Valentina dragged a chair closer to the desk.

"Just that they both had items from the new antique store."

"What about what Dom said? Were they dating anyone? It says here that Tracy had a note in her datebook." She underlined the sentence with her red nails. "At the time the murder may have happened she had a date with 'A. Man,' or did she just mean 'a man'? Maybe she was going on a blind date?"

"I did some checking and she went out with Nathan, one of the cops here, a few times but nothing serious. I've got Arlo asking around about Amy." He twirled a Cartier pen around his fingers. "Val, you were great with finding out who was bothering Madison and the other businesses in town. See what you can find out this time. Anyone just move to town in the last few months who sends up a flag. Check out this antique guy also. I tapped Ryan's phone—"

"What? You tapped his phone?" Thank goodness she hadn't sent any suggestive photos, not that she ever would.

"Not his personal one, just the department's." He flicked through the stack of papers again.

Valentina slapped the back of his head as only a sister could get away with. "As the family's lawyer, I did not hear that."

He swatted her away as if she was a bug. "Here it is. Follow up on this conversation he had with the police department in McGraw County. See what you can find out about who Elizabeth LaGrander-Davis was sleeping with in town."

She read through the transcripts. Something didn't add up. "I'm on it." Using the spare computer in Roman's office, she sent off a work order to a private detective they had on the payroll and sent him down South.

After about an hour, Valentina stopped, removed her reading glasses, and asked her brother, "What do you know about etorphine?"

"Never heard of it," Roman answered.

"I have," Dominic, who was studying the reports as well, said. "It's what that serial killer used on that TV show."

Val and Roman both stared.

"You know, the one with the blood spatter guy who worked for the police department and then he hunted down and killed the bad guys who got away." It was one of the few times she'd ever seen him smile. "I loved that show."

"Where do you get it?" Roman typed the drug name into his laptop.

"What?" Valentina glanced back and forth between the two.

"Etorphine."

"Oh, it's used on animals, so I would think only veterinarians would have something like that." Dom got up from the leather couch and wandered over to his boss's desk.

"It says here it's used for big animals like rhinos and elephants," Roman explained. "I can't see any vet places even needing something like that here."

"We aren't too far away from that circus place. They might have it around just in case they need to work on an elephant." Unfortunately, if they started calling vet clinics and asking about etorphine, it might raise some red flags.

"Good point."

"There you are." Madison strolled into the room.

Roman quickly gathered all the crime reports, put them in a folder, and locked them in a desk drawer.

She glanced back and forth between the three. "I know the drill. Don't ask."

"We were just finishing up." Valentina exited out of everything on her laptop and closed the lid.

"Great. Then you can see the dress I've designed for you." She clapped her hands together in front of her chest. It had always been a dream of Maddy's to be a clothing designer but she never wanted to leave her beloved hometown. When possible, she still liked to sketch and make gowns for her friends' special events or weddings.

"I'm thrilled, but what is it for?" It was a good bet that Ryan might be the one to someday walk her down the aisle, but that was a long way off. They just started dating.

"The Snowflake Ball," she squealed.

"I don't know if I'm going to get all dressed up. I really should be working it. I need to put in more time at Firenza." Would Ryan ask her to go? The man would probably have to work that night anyway.

"Of course you are dressing up. You have to. Now come see what I made for you."

So excited was Madison that she jumped up and down a few times. Val narrowed her eyes at her brother as his gaze zeroed in on his wife's bouncing breasts.

"Lead the way." She shook her head at Roman and followed his wife out the door and into her sewing room. Fabric and sketches were everywhere, but one thing in the room stood out.

"It's stunning." As if in a trance, Valentina carefully stepped over boxes, gloves, and boning that littered the floor. There in front of her on a mannequin was the most beautiful dress she had ever seen. It was a red strapless silk gown. The bodice was fitted, as was the skirt, but the back flared out into a small train.

Before even being asked, Valentina stripped out of her clothes and slipped it on. It fit like a glove. Stepping in front of the floor-length mirror, she felt like a princess, and not just a mafia one. The color reminded her of the bunny costume and her cheeks flushed.

"You must be thinking of a certain officer." Madison hugged her shoulder and looked at their reflection in the glass. "You're going to take his breath away."

"How much? I want it." She turned and kissed Maddy on the cheek.

"It's free. I'm happy to have such a pretty sister-in-law to give it to."

Valentina waltzed around the room. "I can't wait to wear it, but what if he doesn't want to go with me?"

"Any man would be honored to take you to the ball." Roman stood at the door. "You look lovely, Valentina."

"I don't want just any man." She stopped in front of the mirror and stiffened. This time it was her brother who stood next to her, staring back.

"I've never encouraged this. He's a police offer and we operate on the edge of the law, but if Ryan is the one you want, you have my blessing." He rested a hand on her shoulder. Tears threatened to fall as she turned and wrapped him in her arms. Her family may not have been perfect, but they did love her.

Chapter Eighteen

Ryan

Ryan had smiled more in the last two weeks than he had in his entire life. The woman in front of him chatted away but he hadn't heard a word she said, he only had eyes for the one waiting at the table.

"Sir, did you want your change?" the barista repeated.

"No, thanks. Just put it in the tip jar." He took a cup in each hand.

"Here you go." He set Val's drink in front of her. "Sure you don't want a muffin or anything?"

"No, I want to fit into my dress." She took a sip and moaned. "This is heaven."

The sweet sound that came from her lips stirred him below the belt. It was hard to concentrate when she was around. At least once a day they'd seen each other. Sometimes it was just for morning coffee, other times they went out for dinner or just watched a game. They were dating. Slowly. It was the way he wanted it. Valentina deserved better than a *wham bam, thank you, ma'am* date. She was special. She was the real deal and he craved her for a lifetime, not just a night.

He let the comment about the dress slip on purpose. The Snowflake Ball was only a few nights away and Valentina had dropped several hints about wanting to go, but so far he'd ignored them. Sure, he was taking her, but he was waiting for the perfect moment to ask. If he didn't have to work at the last minute that is.

"Anything planned for the rest of the week? Say, like, Friday night?" Her graceful fingers stirred the coffee with a tiny red straw.

"Still not sure if I have to work or not." Thankfully, there hadn't been any more murders. They still weren't any closer to finding the killer, though, either. There were no prints, no witnesses, and being in a small town, no video surveillance.

His phone buzzed. It was a text from Danny. A dark cloud seemed to come over the room and it was hard to breath. They'd found another one. It was like a hit to the stomach and he pushed his coffee aside.

Valentina put a hand over his. "What is it?"

"I've got to go." He kissed her cheek and she held tight to his hand.

"It's happened again. Hasn't it?" Pain shown in her dark eyes and her lower lip trembled.

He nodded and kissed her hand before letting go. "I'll tell Dom to come sit with you." The guy was out in the car, reading a book of all things.

"No, I'll leave now."

After seeing Val safely to her bodyguard, Ryan

drove to the crime scene. There were already several cars in the parking lot of the veterinary clinic. He left his coat in the car and hurried to the front entrance. It was getting colder and colder but right now it didn't matter one bit.

He never had cause to visit the place except to drop Milo off for his shots. The clinic had the usual hospital cleaning supplies smell mixed with a hint of animal urine.

Dr. Bob was on his phone, speaking quietly, but looked up when he noticed Ryan and nodded. He was visibly upset, as was everyone else in the place. A tearful worker dressed in scrubs hugged another person by the door.

Ryan walked into the back room and a body lay in front of some pet cages. A poodle whined and wagged its tail. If only the pooch could talk. The place was a mess. Drawers were pulled out, the refrigerator door was open, and some cupboard doors were even yanked from the hinges.

"Same as before," Danny whispered in his ear. "Same needle mark in the neck. Doc here declared her dead." Each victim had been drugged, but killed a different way. Etorphine was what the medical examiner called it, an extremely powerful animal tranquilizer, although it was used on humans in some countries. "Maybe the bastard tore the place apart in search of more etorphine." Danny carefully turned the victim's wrist so that he could see the face. "Looks like her watch was smashed in the struggle. It stopped at seven oh three."

"Son of a bitch." Running his fingers through his hair, Ryan shook his head. "We have to find this guy. The town can't handle another death." Families had lost loved ones and everyone was on edge. Scared to go out and live life like they normally did. Just when things had finally calmed down a little in the local news, a third murder was going to put everyone in a panic. "Who found the body?"

Danny looked at her notes. "The girl out front. Arianne Manning."

Arianne, the badge bunny he'd turned down for the date? "I'll go talk to her." Sure enough, when he went out front, it was Arianne sitting in one of the waiting room chairs. Her arms and legs were crossed.

"Hi, Arianne. Mind if I talk to you for a moment?"

"Yes, of course." Arianne scooted her chair over and he sat down next to her.

"I hear you found the body. Could you tell me what happened?"

"I saw the lights on so I went inside. I called out but no one answered. I thought it was kind of weird so I looked around." Her hands shook. She interlocked her fingers and laid them on her lap. There were beads of sweat on her forehead.

"Can I get you some water?" Ryan stood up.

"Yes, that would be great. I'm just very upset." She fidgeted and rocked back and forth.

"That's understandable. I'll be right back." Paper cup in hand, he returned with some water from the bubbler and gave it to Arianne. "So when you didn't see anyone, what did you do?"

"I, uh, I heard dogs barking in the back so I went

to look. There she was, lying on the floor, clutching her chest."

"Clutching her chest? Was she alive?" That didn't make sense.

"No. No. She wasn't moving. Just lying there like this." Arianne brought her hands up in front of her chest.

"You're sure?" The victim had her arms by her side when Ryan got to the scene.

"Yes, positive." The shaken woman nodded vigorously.

"You didn't try to move or revive her?" The victim had somehow changed position if what Arianne said was true.

"No. I just left to go get help. I was scared."

"Did you see anyone else around? Any cars in the lot?" Ryan took a visual count of the vehicles outside.

"Yes, a van. It was black, dark grey. I don't remember."

He jotted down the description, wondering if the van belonged to Davis. "Any others?"

"No. Just mine and another car. I assumed it belonged to the person inside." She took a sip of the water.

Never had he felt so hopeless. Another death with not much to go on. "If you think of anything, please give us a call." He took out a business card for the department and handed it to her.

Grabbing her purse, she stood up and accepted the card. "I will. Thanks. Is it okay to go now?"

"Sure." Walking over to the entrance, he opened the front door for her. "One more thing before you go."

She hurried out in the cold and Ryan followed.

"Do you have a dog?" he hollered after her.

"What? No, why?" She struggled with the zipper of her coat.

"Just wondering why you were here." He put his hands in his pockets.

"Am I a suspect now? I didn't do anything. I'm the one who called the police." Arianne gave up on the zipper, stomped her foot, and put her gloves on.

"I didn't say that. You came here for a reason so I didn't want you to forget to get what you came in here for." And why so early? Judging by the hours listed on the door, she had arrived at least an hour before the clinic opened.

"If you must know, I was driving by and, like I said, I saw a car here. Since I can't get equipment yet for my fitness center, I thought I would use the space to collect clothes for charity. You know coats, boots, and gloves. Stuff like that." Her cheeks turned pink from the cold and little puffs of air escaped as she talked.

"That's sounds like a great idea. I will ask around and see if anyone wants to donate." Valentina had a kind heart, she'd be happy to help with something like that.

"Can I go now? I'm freezing." Her teeth chattered.

"It's only forty degrees out, what are you going to do when it hits thirty below?" Winter was hard on locals, let alone people from the South.

"I'll get used to it. That's what everyone keeps telling me." Arianne let out one more wisp of air.

"Are we done now?"

"Yeah." He studied her as she rushed to her car. The plates were from Georgia, just like the ones on Edward's van. Her story didn't jive. When he got back to the station, he'd run a check on those plates. "One more thing."

She stopped. "Now what?"

"I need you to stop at the station later." Ryan walked to where she stood bouncing from one foot to the other.

"Why? I gave your my statement."

"We need to get your fingerprints so that all we find at the scene are accounted for."

"Fine," she grumbled, "I'll do it after lunch."

Once Arianne drove off, an ambulance pulled in. They'd be taking the body to the hospital morgue and the medical examiner would meet them there. It hurt just as bad as the first one. A young life cut needlessly short. He'd catch this murderer if it was the last thing he did.

Ryan reentered the vet clinic and pulled Dr. Bob aside. "What's going on, Bob?"

"I don't know. I don't know who would be doing such a thing but it has to stop soon." The man teared up. "Alyssa is the daughter of a friend of mine. What am I going to tell them? What do I say?"

He placed a hand on the man's shoulder. "We'll do it together, okay?"

Dr. Bob took out a handkerchief and blew his nose. "Thanks." He nodded and wiped the back of his hand across his forehead.

"Tell me what happened. Why was Alyssa here so early?" Ryan took out his notebook again.

"One of the dogs that just had surgery needed to be checked on so she volunteered to come in at seven, give him his meds, and let him out for a bit."

"So she opened up the place?"

"Yes, but she would have locked back up once inside. We always leave the door locked except for during business hours." Yet Arianne had come inside. Had the killer run out and left it that way?

"When I got here, Arianne was by her car. As soon as I got out of the truck, she started screaming that someone was dead inside." The man rubbed his jaw. "I never expected this. Never."

"Was she dead when you found her?"

"Yes."

"How was Alyssa laying when you arrived? Did you move her or try to resuscitate her, give CPR?"

"No, she's as I found her. Arms by her side. I checked for a pulse but there was none. The body had already cooled. It was too late to do anything." The doctor pulled out a chair and sat down. "Her eyes were open." As a coroner, the man had seen death many times, but it was different when it was someone you knew.

"What time did you get here?"

"A little before eight."

"Was anything else out of place?"

"I didn't notice. Wait." The doctor suddenly stood up and rushed to the back room. "I saw in the autopsy report that the Housewife Killer is using etorphine." Dr. Bob pulled open a cupboard. "This is always locked."

"Don't touch anything." Danny rushed over. Inside the cupboard was a mess. Bottles and boxes

179

were tipped over. "Is this where the etorphine is kept?"

"Yes. We only have one bottle because of the circus elephants. It's very potent. Here it is." He pointed at a little container.

"That's a package of suppositories." Danny took her pen and peeked in the box.

"When I read the report, I put it in there. If someone tried to get in and steal it, they hopefully wouldn't find it." Clever. "I guess they didn't realize there'd be no reason to lock up laxatives, so it worked."

"Did any of the girls working here know that?" Ryan glanced at Alyssa, who was being lifted onto a gurney. His heart ached at the loss and it was his determination to catch the killer that kept him on his feet.

"No, and only the other doctor and I have a key."

"And where is your partner now?"

"She comes in the afternoon."

"Has the drug been tampered with in anyway?" Danny studied the bottle that had been the killer's target.

Dr. Bob checked it over and shook his head. "No, it looks fine."

"Do you have any security cameras here?"

He shook his head and leaned against the counter as he witnessed them putting a sheet over Alyssa's body. "No, but I'm ordering some today."

"Ryan. Look what I just found." Danny held up another day of the week towel.

Chapter Nineteen

It was the night of the Snowflake Ball and he was still working. So much for his plans to take Valentina out, but the sooner this man was caught, the better. According to the ME, Alyssa had been injected with far more than the other two girls. The high dosage had caused her to go into cardiac arrest. That may have explained why Arianne said the woman had been clutching her chest in pain. But why were her arms by her side when they found her?

The chief said Ryan could take off early and that was the plan. Hopefully, he would get to the ball before the dance ended. If he'd learned anything in the last few weeks, it was that life was short.

With a groan he put all the papers on his desk in a folder and shoved them in a drawer. They had no leads and no fingerprints. The footprint they'd found at Tracy's trailer belonged to the guy who reads the electrical meters. Never in his career had he felt so helpless, but he wasn't giving up. Ryan had requested photos and names of any other possible victims in unsolved cases in Georgia but time was running out. Hopefully, he'd have them by tomorrow.

There was nothing else he could do at the moment, but that didn't mean he couldn't stop living. With so much bad in the world, it was time for some beauty, and that meant only one thing— Valentina.

It didn't take long to get dressed and be on the way to Firenza. On the way, he stopped at the flower shop and picked up a bouquet of red roses. He didn't know Valentina well enough to know all her likes but she seemed to enjoy the flowers he'd sent her the first time. Driving down a side street, he spied a man backing his lawnmower out of the garage so he pulled over and stopped.

"Where you headed?" he shouted over the sound of the mower, and finally had to get out of the truck so the man would see him. The older guy sported a suit and tie. "Lucky, what the hell are you doing?"

"Probably the same thing you're doing. Going to the dance." He idled in the driveway.

"On your lawnmower? It's too damn cold and dark out to do that."

"Well, some dumbass took away my license so I can't drive anything else," Lucky spat.

"Put that thing back in the garage and this dumbass will give you ride." Ryan pointed to the still open garage door.

"Well, all right, but only because I want to look good for the ladies. You never know, I might meet the next Mrs. Bauer tonight." Not waiting for a response, Lucky revved the engine, parked it in the shed, and shut the door.

Ryan shook his head and waited in the warm truck for the crazy old coot.

The first thing Lucky noticed in the truck was the flowers. "You get them for me?" He settled in and buckled his seatbelt.

"No, someone better looking." They backed out of the driveway and headed off down the street.

"That could be anyone, but I'm thinking it's the pretty lawyer who just moved here. I've heard the rumors that you were sporting her around town. If I were a few years younger, I might give you a run for your money."

"If you were a few years younger, I'd be worried," he teased, and the old man laughed. "So, how did you get all those ladies to marry you, Lucky?"

"I asked them, simple as that." So much for getting advice from the older generation. Things used to be so much easier in the old days, it seemed.

"Simple as that, huh?" Things might be a little more complicated with Valentina and her family. "What if she's from a very traditional family?"

"Then ask the father before you ask her. If you can win them over first, there's no way she can say no." Everything seemed uncomplicated to Lucky.

"What if they still won't accept you?" Ryan pressed.

"Then don't give them a choice." Lucky placed his elbow on the armrest. "I know about her family, everybody does. It's like the movie with Brando. Make an offer they can't pass up."

He pondered the advice as they pulled into the driveway of Firenza. That would be a last resort. Roman would come around. All he cared about was his sister's happiness. It was ridiculous to be thinking about this stuff already anyway.

It was like a winter wonderland driving down the lane to Valentina's club, with white Christmas lights hanging from the trees. The parking lot was packed. Ladies in long dresses and men in tuxes walked arm and arm to the building. After finally finding a parking spot, they both exited the vehicle.

"So how am I going to get home?" Lucky wondered.

Flowers in one hand, Ryan dug in his pocket and handed the guy a twenty. "Take a cab. No offense, but I'm hoping to take someone more beautiful home."

The guy didn't argue, just took the money and stuffed it in his jacket. "I know I give you crap, Donavan, but you're all right." The both started walking. "I hope you get the girl."

"Thanks." Ryan glanced up at the night sky. "Me too."

Valentina

It hurt like hell that Ryan was working, but he had an important job to do. The murders hadn't kept people from attending the ball. If anything, it was as if people wanted to get out and be with others. They had extra security just in case.

Tyler and his mom, Shelly, were doing a great job. Shelly served drinks and Tyler bused tables and helped serve hors d'oeuvres. Valentina made sure to compliment them on a job well done. The kid was a great help. He always showed up on time for work and never said no to any task. His mother had blossomed as well. It was even rumored that the cook and she were taking a shine to each other.

Madison and Roman danced just about every dance. The two only had eyes for each other. Seeing them together made Valentina's heart ache even more. How she wished Ryan was there. Everyone on the force was putting in more hours to try to find the killer.

What would he think if he knew she'd just reviewed the same reports that he must have been going over? The private detective they had in Georgia hoped to get them a list soon of who Elizabeth LaGrander-Davis may have been seeing, as well as more info on any other unsolved cases in the state.

"May I have this dance?" a voice asked behind her.

Valentina grinned and turned around. Smiling up at her was a grey-haired gentleman with a sparkle in his eyes. "Yes, thank you. I'd be honored to." She looped her arm around his and he guided her to the dance floor. The song ended and a waltz began. "What is your name?"

"Lucky Bauer, and it's a pleasure to be dancing with such a beautiful lady as you."

"Well, thank you, Mr. Bauer." The guy was a flirt, she could tell right way, but he still made her giggle. "You are quite the charmer, and quite the dancer, I must say." He was very light on his feet and all too soon the song was over.

"I would like another one, but I think there's someone else you'd rather twirl around the dance floor with." He gave a slight bow.

"Oh really?" She lifted her eyebrow. "And who might that be?"

"The guy who brought me here so I wouldn't have to drive my lawnmower in the cold."

Lucky pointed to a handsome man by the front door. Valentina took a step forward. Her heart leapt in her chest. It was Ryan. Dressed in a suit and holding a bouquet of red roses.

"Thank you for the dance, miss. Now don't keep him waiting," Lucky said so only she could hear.

She kissed the guy on the cheek and hurried over to where her prince was waiting. He looked like royalty in his black tie and crisp white shirt. Valentina's steps slowed as she got closer. The past week, Ryan had stopped shaving like most men in the area did during hunting season. Just thinking about that rough jawline along her skin made her knees weak.

"I thought you had to work." Her smile was so wide, her cheeks hurt. Her arms couldn't get around his waist fast enough. The warmth from his body heated her from the inside out.

"I did, but I wasn't going to miss seeing you." Valentina blushed as his eyes traveled slowly from her face to the tip of her red shoes. He whistled. "Wow, you look amazing."

"It's the dress. Madison made it for me." She spun around.

"No, it's definitely you." Ryan dropped a kiss to her lips and they nearly crushed the flowers as they embraced again. "You'd look beautiful no matter what you had on. Oh, these are for you."

"I love them." They smelled heavenly. "Thank you so much, and thank you for being here." She looped her arm around his waist and led him to a table.

"Believe me, I wouldn't miss a chance to be with you for anything in the world."

Valentina was officially the host of the party, but with such great employees, she was able to relax and spend time with the one she loved.

Loved? When did that happen? Ever since they'd sat down, Ryan had kept her hand in his. His thumb caressed her palm and just that light touch was enough to create flutters in her belly. They even danced a few times. Ryan claimed to not be a good dancer but he had all the right moves to her.

"Hey, Val." Madison came up behind her while Ryan went to get them some drinks. "If you guys want to go, I can finish up here. Roman had to go take care of some business so I am looking for something to do. Stephanie is here also." Valentina noticed the blonde behind her. Stephanie had been running Madison's bridal store ever since she and Roman got married.

"Hi, Stephanie. I didn't notice you dancing."

The girl twirled a strand of long gold hair around her finger. "I doubt you would notice anyone tonight except the guy you're with," she teased, and nodded in Ryan's direction.

"That's true, but what about you?" Valentina glanced over to where Dominic stood against the wall. His eyes were locked on Steph. "Any guys catch your fancy?"

"Heck no." Her response was quick, too quick. From what she'd seen, the girl never went out and dated less than Valentina had.

"What about Dom? He's a handsome man." He was dressed in a suit and his long hair was tied in back. He was a fine-looking guy, that was for sure. Without his usual lumberjack attire the man looked like a male model who had just stepped out of a high-end fashion magazine.

His face flushed red when Steph peered his way and Dom quickly glanced elsewhere. Madison and Valentina eyes locked. To say the pair had a strong dislike for each other whenever they were in the same room was putting it lightly. Yet the two were often found peeking at the other when they thought no one noticed. What was the saying? There was a fine line between love and hate.

"I'd rather dance with the devil, but that's what he is, isn't he? A demon with long hair," she spat, and planted her hands on her hips.

"Come on, there must be someone here you want to be with." Madison had not given up on finding her friend a mate.

It was slight, but Stephanie's gaze flashed in Dom's direction before drifting to the floor. "No, I'm just not interested. I'll probably just go home, if that's okay. I'm tired." Her hand rose to her mouth to hide a yawn. "It's a busy time of year at the art center." She volunteered there when she wasn't working at Bells and Bows.

"That's fine if you want to go home, but I'm not letting you leave alone," Madison said, and motioned Dominic over. "Roman doesn't want any woman going home unattended. Not until that killer is caught."

The poor girl went pale and grabbed Madison's arm. "No, not him. Can't Arlo take me?"

"Arlo's busy. Dom will take good care of you. Don't worry."

Valentina noticed Steph's cheeks turn pink and added, "I trust him with my life and so does my brother. You have nothing to be concerned about."

Valentina's handyman and part-time bodyguard weaved through the crowd as smooth as any dancer. The man's eyes were focused on Steph the whole time as she half hid behind Maddy.

"Dominic, I need you to take Stephanie home and see her safely inside. Check out the place too and make sure everything is good before you leave."

He nodded but his face remained stoic. Madison gave him her friend's address and gently shoved the shy girl in his direction.

"Really, Madison, I don't need someone to go with me." The girl shook her head and planted her feet. "I'm not a child."

"Three women have been murdered and whoever did it is still out there," Valentina insisted.

"You'll be safe with me." Dominic smiled, and all three women turned in his direction. The man was not a talker, hated spending time around people, and saying something meant to calm another was unheard of. When he held his hand out to her, Val's and Maddy's mouths dropped. Stephanie didn't seem to noticed their reaction and with great hesitation took one small step forward and then another. The Caponelli cleaner tucked her small hand in the crook of his elbow and led her from the room.

"What the hell was that?" Valentina uttered.

"I don't know, but I can't wait to find out tomorrow." Madison folded her arms across her chest.

"What did I miss?" Ryan had returned with two glasses of champagne. He held one out to Madison. Would you like some champagne?"

"No, thanks. Since Valentina wants to go home with you, I said I would take over." She winked at Ryan and Val's face flushed. Her friend just set her up, but she didn't mind, not in the least.

He didn't wait for a denial. "Thanks. Let's go, then." Ryan put his arm around Valentina and quickly guided her out of the ballroom.

"What's the rush?" Her heart was giddy. Finally, they would be together, all night long.

"I don't want you to change your mind."

She'd barely gotten her coat on before they were out the door.

Light bits of moisture hit her face. "Look, it's snowing." With arms outstretched, she twirled around and tried to catch a snowflake on her tongue. Before she knew it, her feet were out from under her and she was in the air. Ryan had picked her up and was carrying her toward his truck.

"I didn't want you to fall and break your pretty neck." He kissed her forehead.

"I've already fallen." Her finger traced his jawline. "For you."

Chapter Twenty

Ryan's was a modest single-story home on the edge of town. That fact barely registered as her only thoughts were on him and the night ahead. Everything had been leading up to this moment. She would finally be his.

As soon as they were out of the vehicle, he lifted her up in his arms again.

"I can walk." She looped an arm around his neck.

"I know, but the snow is making it slippery and, as usual, you are not wearing practical shoes." He kissed her forehead again.

"I know for a fact that you love my shoes." Snowflakes floated down and melted on her cheeks.

"I do." He set her down safely in front of the door as he reached in his pocket for the key. "I can't wait to see you wearing nothing but." His voice was husky and her heartbeat accelerated.

As soon as the door opened, she was swept inside. Her coat thrown across a chair and her purse dropped on the couch. Again, she was lifted off her feet. "Put me down." He carried her to the bedroom. "I've not been carried this much since I was a kid."

He carefully set her on the big king-size bed. "I'm afraid you bring out the caveman in me," Ryan joked, and removed his suitcoat. The man was dashing in his suit but it was the uniform that made her weak in the knees.

Valentina rose and unzipped the back of her dress. She may be daring in the daylight but this was a whole new ballgame. Her fingers shook as she slipped the dress past her hips and it fell to the floor in a pool of red silk. The heat of his intense gaze caused her nipples to peak. All she had on was a red thong and the red high heels he loved.

"Wow." He just stood and stared for a moment before shaking his head and stepping close to her. "You're too stunning to be legal." He took off his shirt so fast a few buttons went flying about the room. The guy had to work out because he was ripped. When he pulled her into his arms, he held her so tight she could feel his strength. The warmth of his chest pressed against her breasts caused a pool of heat to settle in her belly. She wanted this, needed this.

His lips were all over. Her mouth, her neck, her breasts. The roughness of his beard was sure to leave a mark and she relished the burn. Valentina ached for it to never stop. Each part of her flesh wanted and demanded more of his attention. The first time his mouth touched her nipple, her knees went weak. If it weren't for the tight grip he had around her waist she'd surely have slipped to the floor. Her fingers threaded through his thick hair. It was soft and smelled like his shampoo.

Before she knew it, he lifted her back in his arms and laid her gently on the bed. A girl could get use to that. Valentina wiggled on the plush covers under the heat of his gaze. Ryan kicked off his shoes before unzipping his pants and removing them, his briefs, and socks in record speed.

"I can't wait to make you mine." He nuzzled her ear. It tickled and she squirmed.

"Then do it. We have all night to go slow." She pulled his face to hers. "I want you now." So much for being shy in the bedroom. If she brought out his caveman, he was bringing forth her femme fatale.

He settled between her legs. His hair roughed skin against her smooth skin sent goosebumps to her toes. Ryan hesitated. "Is this the awkward moment where I ask if I need to use a condom?"

"I'm clean, on the pill, and the few times I've had sex were a long time ago."

"I'm clean too and I am going to make you forget the names of anyone you ever slept with before." He reached between her legs and she gasped.

"You already did." Valentina reached for his hard length. It was smooth, warm, and pulsing to her touch. "Make me yours now," she demanded.

He removed her hand and settled himself at her core. In one swift thrust he took her to the moon and back. Her world spun as he moved. Valentina climbed to the skies, soaring higher and higher until she hit a star and came floating back to earth. Ryan whispered words of love the whole time. He groaned and came crashing down beside her, gathering her into his arms.

"You're mine now. I'm going to spend the rest of the night, and the rest of my life if you want me to, showing you how much I want you."

"Prove it." Her challenge just made him smile, and he spent the rest of the night doing just that.

Valentina tiptoed across the floor but the old hardwood creaked with every step. As soon as she dove back into bed, he grabbed her.

"Trying to sneak out on me?" he teased, and cradled her in his arms.

"Would I be back in bed if I was?" So much for sneaking to the bathroom, the guy didn't miss a thing. She wrapped one of her legs around his.

"No, but I can't stand the thought of ever being in this bed alone again."

It sounded like heaven but it was still too soon to move in together. "I don't like the thought of that either. What do you want to do today?" She snuggled in close. His skin was so smooth and warm. Leaving the bed again would be torture.

"I have to work a few hours and see if we've gotten anything new on the Housewife Killer. I won't rest until the man is caught and in jail. Even if it means I have to sacrifice a few hours with my woman." He nuzzled her neck and kissed her before getting out of bed.

Her heart nearly burst from her chest when he said the words *his woman*. "Well, as much as I love the dress I wore last night, I could use some clothes also."

"Borrow some of mine," Ryan said as he pulled on a pair of boxer briefs.

"How about this?" Valentina had slipped on his police uniform shirt and snuck up behind him. His eyes widened in the reflection in the dresser mirror.

"Damn, if that isn't the hottest thing I've ever seen." He turned around and rewarded her with a panty melting kiss. Ryan groaned when the kiss ended. "You are making this really hard to leave."

"I know, I know. I'll stop. I want you to catch this guy just as bad as you do." In the light of day, she noticed a framed photo on his dresser. It was of a happy couple with a young boy. She picked it up. "Is this you and your parents?" The little boy had to be him. Even at that young age he had what it took to grow up to be a heartbreaker.

"Yeah, it is." He took the picture from her hand and set it back in its spot.

"You want to talk about it?" She laid her head on his shoulder and wrapped an arm around his waist.

"No, but I will." Ryan took her hand, led her back to the bed, and they took a seat. "I don't know how much you know about want happened."

"I know he was a district attorney trying to hunt down organized crime and that he was targeting mob members before his death."

"Yes, but they didn't kill him. When I was older, I searched every report, talked to everyone who knew them. There had been no threats. No bounty on him. He shot my mother in the head and then killed himself. A murder-suicide." His voice cracked. "It was his gun, his prints on the gun. What kind of a bastard does that?"

It was obvious that the pain had never lessened. The thought of him as a young boy having suffered such a loss was like a hit to the gut. "Are you sure that's what happened?"

"Believe me, I checked every report, every file that I could get my hands on. Some are still closed but the fact remains, he killed her. We were a happy family. I know we were." His fists opened and closed. "It devastated me. Changed me. After that, I never wanted to get close to anyone for fear of their loss. I locked myself down. What if there is some evil part of my father that carried down to me?" He choked. It took a lot to admit that to her, she was sure.

"I'm so sorry, but I don't believe there is one bad part of you." She rubbed his arm.

"There are bad parts in everyone. Would you not kill to protect the ones you love? I know for a fact your brother has."

Valentina knew better than to admit that was true, but her brother had killed a maniac who threatened Madison and another girl the man had abused. Ryan's phone buzzed. He patted Valentina's leg and rose to answer it.

After ending the call, he turned to Val and said, "That was Danny. We received some photos of women who went missing or were found dead in McGraw County." He pulled on a long-sleeve Henley, his uniform, and gun belt. Valentina dressed in her walk of shame dress from last night. At least it was still early and most of the town was probably still asleep or in church.

"Great. I hope it gives you more clues. Do you think the antique dealer is still involved?"

"No, it turns out his wife was cheating on him with the police chief. Her family wanted her death covered up, so everyone kept quiet about her affairs. He wasn't even in the state when one of the women was killed, and he was at a chamber of commerce breakfast when the vet clinic was broken into the other day."

"Who could it be?" The room was warm but a chill ran through her veins. They had to find the person, and fast.

"That's what I hope to find out." Ryan attached his police utility belt to his pants belt with some keepers, put on a coat, and they were out the door.

Ryan

There was a nice coating of snow on the road but his truck handled it just find. It being a Sunday, the snowplows were not out as much as they would be during a weekday. As he drove into the Lake Genoa Police Department parking lot, he waved at the snow removal driver. Danny's and Nate's cars were there and a few others that he recognized. The radio was calling for at least a foot of snow. It was early for that much but it had happened in the past. One Halloween night they got twenty-eight inches.

Getting out of bed that morning was one of the

hardest things he'd ever done. Spending the night with Valentina was heaven, and it was hell to be apart. It was better than he dreamed it could be. Just the thought of her soft skin against his was hot enough to defrost the windows of his truck.

She was his future. His life. The main reason he wanted to catch the monster that had threatened the town. Glancing at the clock, he counted the hours until they would be together again. At least she was safe at her house right now.

He pulled his collar up to fight off the snow and chilly air. The heat of the building hit his face the moment he walked through the door.

"Hey, Nate." Ryan met up with his coworker as he headed to their meeting room. The chief had sent a message that he wanted a meeting with whoever was working the morning shift.

"Ryan. Did you have a good time last night?" He gave him a nudge with his elbow.

"I did. How about yourself? Who's the girl I saw you with?" He'd seen them last night but was so focused on Val that he didn't want to talk to anyone else.

"Amy. Amy Foster." His eyes seemed to shine brighter than ever before at the mention of his new girl.

"Don't know her." They reached the room and Ryan held the door open for him. "She from around here?"

"No, Delavan. She works at her parents' dry cleaner store."

Something nagged at the back of Ryan's mind. What were the chances that there were two girls named Amy who worked at laundry businesses?

Chief Schneider was standing at the front of the room, asking everyone to take a seat. He had salt and pepper hair and thick glasses, and was sharper on his game than anyone there. "I know many of you have been working long hours trying to find the Housewife Killer. Danny has some more things that came in on the fax from McGraw County. She's handing out copies so let's all go over these and see if anything stands out."

Danny rounded the room, giving everyone copies, but she stopped when she got to Ryan. She tossed his in front of him and took a seat beside him. "You've got lipstick on your cheek." It was said loud enough for everyone to hear and all eyes turned his way as he wiped at his face with the back of his hand. Hoots and hollers followed.

"Just messing with you." She punched him in the arms.

"Dammit, Dan, you're such a pest." But he had to admit he liked her.

"I'm happy for you." This time she spoke only so only he could hear. The sincere expression showed that she meant it.

"Thanks." Ryan nodded and opened the file in front of him. The woman was becoming the closest thing to a younger sister he'd ever had and it was a good feeling. It would be great to have a family, even if they weren't blood related. His coworkers were like his kin.

"Okay," Chief Schneider said, quieting everyone, "now that everyone knows Ryan's got a lady friend, let's get back to work. Ryan, get everyone up to date on where we're at."

Ryan shared with the group the story of Elizabeth LaGrander-Davis and her relationship with Officer Moore in Dixon, Georgia. There were crime scene photos of a few women who had similar unexplained deaths. One had gone into cardiac arrest just as the victim at the vet clinic had. Another had been beaten with a bat, yet still had a dose of etorphine in her system.

Next, he read the bios and statements from friends and family. One victim had just become engaged to a police officer on the force.

"Wait a second." Ryan's chair screeched as he slid back. "I think I see a connection here and you're not going to like it."

Chapter Twenty-One

Valentina

If it was possible, Valentina was pretty sure she'd been walking on air ever since Ryan left. The head spinning kiss he left her with would have to last until he returned. He'd only agreed to leave her at her home alone because of the security system and cameras. After a quick shower and some coffee from one of the coffee makers she'd been gifted, she dressed in leggings, a sweater, and some boots.

Once he was done going through the files from Georgia, Ryan was going to pick up a pizza and they would catch a game. Roman would have those files by now but she just couldn't look at them. Not today. Nothing was going to destroy the bliss she was feeling.

She flipped through the channels to find the time of the game. The one they wanted was on at three. Valentina let out a deep breath and tossed the remote on the couch. Since she'd moved to Genoa there was always something to do—unpacking, going through files, having meetings at Firenza—but today nothing seemed important.

It was like she was waiting on the edge of her seat for Ryan to stroll through the door. The party last night had been a great opportunity for everyone to get out of the house, put on some dressy clothes, and have fun. With the killer still on the loose, everyone was still looking over their shoulders, double locking their doors, and wringing their hands with worry. *Was the person sitting next to me at the Java Shop the Housewife Killer? Was he standing behind me in the line at the Piggy Wiggly? Did he live next door?*

Pushing aside a curtain, she peered down the street. It looked like a snow globe outside. No one was out walking or pushing strollers. Sure, it was a cold, stormy day, but that was nothing to people who just a few years ago lived through the coldest winter in history. It was not uncommon to have a high of fifteen below. It was as if the soul of the town was dying and there was no way to revive it until the killer was caught. Only then could the people breathe again.

The doorbell rang and she nearly jumped out of her skin. He was here already. She hurried to the door and swung it open. "I'm going to have to get you a key so—" Valentina halted. It wasn't Ryan but the woman who had been his date at the western dance. "Uh, hi. Can I help you?"

"Hi, I'm Arianne." She held a gloved hand out to shake. "You must be Valentina. Officer Ryan told me about you."

Reluctantly, Valentina shook the woman's hand.

She didn't know this person from Adam and now she was on her doorstep. Remembering her manners, she invited her in. "It's freezing out, please come in." Arianne stepped inside and stuffed her gloves in her coat pockets. "I didn't mean to stand there like a deer in the headlights, it's just—"

"I know. The Housewife Killer. Believe me, I've been afraid to leave the house except for during the day. I'm sorry to drop in like this but I ran into Ryan when I was at the vet clinic the other day." Her face went white. "I was the one who found that poor woman."

"Oh no." She put a hand over her heart. "I can't imagine. How horrible."

"Yes. It was." Arianne unzipped her coat. "Ryan suggested I contact you."

"Really?" She couldn't think of a reason why Ryan would put them in contact.

"I'm chairing a coat drive for needy kids. I was at the clinic to ask if they would like to donate. Ryan said you had a kind heart and might be willing to help out."

"Of course I would. What do you need me to do?"

"Are you free now? I just got a huge donation and I could sure use some help unpacking and hanging them up."

The clock on the wall said it was only ten. There was still plenty of time to help with the coats and be back for the game. "Sure. Where are they?"

"I rented a place by the old strip mall for my fitness center. I'm still waiting on the equipment to come in so I'm using the space to store everything for the drive. Next week, we are inviting kids from the area to pick out their coats. We'll have games and cake and ice cream for them too."

Maybe she'd misjudged Arianne. Her relationship with Ryan, whatever it may have been, shouldn't affect her helping with a good cause. "I'd be happy to help with that also."

"Oh, thank you. The kids will be so happy. It shouldn't take more than an hour or so to get things set up today. If you want to grab your coat, we can take my car. It's already warm."

"Sure. I'll be right there." Valentina stuffed her phone and keys in her coat, locked the door, and hurried down to the sidewalk where Arianne waited in her car. It would be good to feel useful while she waited for her man to get home. She buckled herself in and they were off. After a few minutes of awkward small chat, they drove past the strip mall. Hardly anyone was at the shops—most of the stores were only open Monday through Sunday. It wasn't too far from home so she could walk back if she wanted to.

"Here we are. I still have the paper covering the windows but I thought we could take that down and put up some decals." They parked and got out of the car.

"Yes, that would be nice."

Arianne unlocked the door and entered the vacant store. She flipped a switch and the fluorescent lights buzzed and flickered to life. A few were out and would need to be replaced before the place opened for business. It took a moment for Valentina's eyes to adjust. The brightness of the

205

snow made it hard to see going into the dim building.

"They dropped the boxes off in the back. We can unpack them there and then bring them out here. I had hoped the tables would be here in time but they won't be in until tomorrow."

"All right. I wish I would have known—we could have brought some over from Firenza." Valentina unzipped her coat.

Arianne pulled out her phone and frowned.

"Is everything okay?" Valentina took a step in her direction.

"Yes, I just have to make a call. Would you mind going in the back and opening the boxes? There should be a boxcutter back there." Her fingers were already moving across the cell screen.

"Sure. I'd be happy too." Valentina took one more look around the empty store before heading to the back room. It would take a lot of work to get this place kid ready by next weekend. Maybe Roman would let her borrow Dom again to at least get some of the lightbulbs changed and fixtures repaired. Her boots clipped on the tile floor as she strode into the empty back room. Where were the boxes? From what Arianne said there should be a ton, but all that was there were a few suitcases and totes. *What the hell?*

Before she could turn around, a plastic bag went over her head. Panic like she'd never known kicked in. She fought like a wildcat, kicking and screaming, but it was no use. Even her fingernails couldn't pierce the bag. Valentina gasped for air and the bag sucked in and out with every breath.

Where was Arianne? Had she been attacked too? Little flashes of light flickered before her eyes, she was getting lightheaded. Her strength faded. Her last thought was of Ryan as she slid to the floor.

Ryan

"What have you got, Ry?" Danny took out a pen and paper.

"What do all, or least most, of these victims have in common?"

"Age and that they were young women." Nate shrugged. "Well, except for LaGrander-Davis, who was in her forties. Still rather young though."

"That's true, but there's more. She was dating, make that having an affair with, a police officer." Everyone just stared as he continued. "One of the victims in Dixon was engaged to a cop. Tracy used to date you, Nate. Right?"

"Yeah, a couple times, but then I met Amy," he added.

"Yes, and what was the name of the second girl killed here? The one who worked at the laundromat?"

Nate's eyes got big. "Amy."

"Right. And your Amy works at a dry cleaners."

"Are you saying that someone is targeting women who date police officers?" The chief rose from the table he was leaning against. "That he killed the wrong Amy?"

"What kind of sick fucker would do that?" Danny asked, disgusted. "And what about the girl killed at the vet clinic? Did anyone here know her?"

They all shook their heads.

"I think that might have been by accident. The killer was searching for more etorphine and wasn't expecting anyone to be there. She was given a lethal dose that sent her into cardiac arrest just like this one here." Ryan flipped through the photos until he came across the one he was searching for. He tapped it with his finger.

"Who is she and was she involved with a man in blue?" Nate stood up and glanced as the photo.

"It says she was single. Same thing might have happened to her as it did to Alyssa. The woman may have been in the wrong place at the wrong time." Ryan scanned the report. "Woman's name was A. Manning."

"What the hell?" Danny snatched it from his hand. "A. Manning as in A. Man?"

A few guys still had blank looks on their faces but Ryan knew the name. "It was in the appointment book of the first victim." He studied the document again. "Name's Arianne Laura Manning."

"Arianne Manning?" Cory, one of the new guys, spoke up. "Isn't that the name of that new chick in town? The one opening the fitness center and trying to get into everyone's pants?"

"Danny, fire up the laptop. Search for any other women who may have disappeared at the time. Enter the names and see what photos come up."

The task seemed to take forever but it was just their impatience. This was the first break in the case and they were so close.

"Nothing. Nothing," Danny said as she punched in the names. "Wait. Take a look at this."

"Holy shit." Ryan bounced out of his seat. The woman who told everyone her name was Arianne Manning was actually Brittany Smith, another woman who had disappeared around the same time as the unsolved murders in Georgia. Arianne—Brittany—must have stolen the license plates from the dead woman's car because they matched her name.

"That's enough for me. Let's bring her in. Danny, you call the judge to get a search warrant," Chief Schneider ordered, and placed his hands on his hips. Excitement ripped through the room. They all wanted to catch the killer, and the fact that she'd been targeting loved ones of police officers just made it that much worse. "Get her home address. Nate and I will go in the front, Cory, you watch the back. No sirens, we don't know if she's the one but don't take any chances. If she is the one, Arianne, or Brittany or whatever her name is, has killed numerous times. Again, don't take any chances."

"Got it."

"Yes, sir."

"Looks like she lives about ten miles out," Danny said as she wrote down the address and handed it to Chief Schneider

Ryan stood up. "Let's go."

"You stay here," the chief instructed. "Keep going over these reports. We're shorthanded with hunting season so I may need you more later. Let these guys bring her in. Danny, you stay here also and find out everything you can on our suspect. I mean everything."

"Already on it." Her fingers attacked the keyboard at warp speed as the guys headed out the door and on the trail of a killer.

Ryan cursed but knew this wasn't the time to argue. This woman needed to be stopped. He'd trail behind in his truck if he had to. He pulled out his phone to send Valentina a text but there was already one there from her.

Hey, handsome. Gone with Arianne to work on the coat drive. See you soon.

His heart dropped to his knees.

Chapter Twenty-Two

Valentina

Voices filtered through the silence and her vision blurred. Valentina tried to raise her hand to her face but it wouldn't move. She couldn't move. Her feet were frozen in place. After a couple of tries, she was finally able to raise her head.

Where was she? The room was bare except for a few bags. *Weren't there more before?* It came back to her in a rush. She'd been with Arianne and then…panic set in. Her hands were duct taped together and her ankles strapped to the legs of a chair. What had happened to Arianne? Were they in the hands of the Housewife Killer? A scream roared in her throat but her mouth was covered with tape.

A gust of cold air flooded the room as a door opened behind her.

"Look who's awake." It was Arianne. Her voice dripped with hate. "Poor, poor Valentina." She reached out a hand and ripped the tape from her captive's mouth.

It burned like a bitch but it awoke Valentina even more. "What's going on? Help me."

"Help you? I'm the one who did this to you." Arianne pointed to her chest with her thumb.

"Why? I don't understand." Where was Ryan? When would he realize she was gone?

"You took something that was mine. You moved into my territory." Her eyes were wide like that of a crazy person.

"What are you talking about? If you want money, just let me call my brother and we'll get you what you need."

"I don't want money, although I did empty your purse of cash." She nodded her head to where Val's handbag lay in a heap on the concrete. "You won't need it anymore. When people take what's mine, they get hurt."

"I don't understand. What you are talking about?" It slowly sunk in that she was in the hands of the Housewife Killer, the one everyone thought was a man. Her skin broke out in a cold sweat.

Arianne pulled up a chair and straddled it. "You don't get it, do you? They never do." She gave Valentina a once over, her eyes going from her toes to her head. "You grew up in some fancy house with nice clothes and a good family."

"I may have grown up in a nice house but that doesn't mean my life was perfect," she countered.

"Well, it was nothing like mine, that is for sure." Arianne's eyes had a glassy look to them.

"What was it like?" Valentina's brain worked overtime to figure out a plan of escape. It was best to keep Arianne talking as long as possible.

"It was just my mom and me. We were what you would call trailer trash. The men who walked through that creaky old screen door were even worse. Pieces of shit every one of them, but that's where the drugs came from to fix her habit. They beat her. They beat me too but I was too young to do anything. Until one day." Her eyes held a faraway look as if she was reliving the nightmare. "Let's see, I had to be seventeen going on thirty. Anyway, a police officer showed up at the door to check on why I hadn't been in school. He took one look at me, my methed out mother, our filthy trailer, and called social services. They had nowhere to place me so the officer and his wife took me in until I was eighteen. It was the only place that I ever felt safe, ever felt clean."

"I'm so sorry. I'm glad he was able to make your life better though." Where was Arianne going with this story?

"I don't want your pity." She rose from the chair and sent it flying across the room.

The woman was a psychopath. Valentina took deep breaths and struggled to remain calm. "So what happened next?" Her fingers were going numb as she tried to pull free from the tape.

"What happened is that he took a job elsewhere and I had to move out. I was on my own again, but before he left he got me a job at the vet clinic there. It was a good job, but as I was leaving one night, I was robbed. I didn't have any money and yet some nutcase decides to freakin' rob me. Punched me in the face and knocked me around." She circled around the room as she talked, her hands flexing

213

with every step. "Again, it was a police officer who came to save me. He waited with me for the ambulance and then visited me in the hospital. The guy was so handsome in his uniform. It was love at first sight."

"Did you go out with him?" The woman's story kept leading toward cops.

"Once. We went out to lunch. He was the perfect gentleman. Asking if I was okay and had a place to stay."

It sounded like the guy was just being nice and making sure she was functioning after her ordeal. He may have been asked to keep an eye on her by his former coworker.

"Did you see him again?"

"I tried, but he kept turning me down. So I followed him. Found out he was engaged. Arianne Manning was her name. She worked at the clinic with me and I never even knew about her involvement with the guy. If he were mine, I'd have shouted it to the world. But she acted like it was nothing to her. I had to get rid of that bitch and then he would be mine."

Arianne had taken that girl's life and name. Valentina let her keep talking, knowing that would give Ryan time to save her. It was clear that she was going to end up like all the others if she wasn't rescued soon.

"I didn't know how to do it, but while watching my favorite television show one night, I got an idea. Etorphine. Just a little dab will do ya. I found that out the hard way. Too much gives a person a heart attack. I like people to know why I'm killing them first, that they were preventing me from having my own safe place. My territory to call my own." The woman was unhinged and Valentina's heart raced.

"Didn't they notice the drug was gone? Isn't it locked up?"

"They rarely use that drug. The vet left his keys for the cabinet behind when he had an emergency call one day. I grabbed it and made a spare while I went to lunch. From then on it was easy. There were no cameras at the clinic. I withdrew the drug with a syringe and no one ever noticed."

Her captor was crazy but smart. "Then what did you do?"

"I went after her. Asked her to help with a charity. Nobody turns that down. I picked her up, stabbed her with the needle, and threw her out of the car and into the river. They searched for a long time but didn't find her. I don't know if they ever did. Her fiancé was too upset over the loss and turned me down whenever I asked him out. I hid her wallet until I left town and then I took her name too."

"Were there others?"

"Of course. The high and mighty Elizabeth LaGrander-Davis was a tramp and stepping out with the local police chief. I followed them to the motel that they use to meet at. After the chief left, I knocked on the door pretending to be housekeeping. When she turned around..." She made a stabbing motion with her hand. "Syringe in the neck and then a pillow over her face. You're lucky. If I still had some, you'd be dead already."

That was a relief, but if someone didn't get to her

soon, she would be dead.

"You're very smart. So are you and Mr. Davis here together? Did he ask you to murder his wife?"

"Hell no. The guy wasn't even in town but he became a suspect. Every time someone went missing, they would question him. When I heard he was leaving town to come here and open shop, I followed. I wore a wig one day and bought a few things to leave at the scenes. We'd never met, but I thought better safe than sorry. And guess what? He became a suspect again." She smiled and snapped her fingers. "I did make one mistake though. The Amy at the laundromat. She was the wrong one."

"What about the girl killed at the vet clinic here?" *I have to keep her talking. Please come save me, Ryan.*

"My supply of etorphine was running low. I didn't think anyone would be there so I picked the locked and went in the back. She surprised me. I had the drug with me and stuck her. The girl went down like a ton of bricks. I wasn't thinking and gave her all I had left." Arianne crossed her arms. "She clutched her chest. Had a heart attack. I searched everywhere but couldn't find more of the drug. I panicked and ran out the front door. Right into the vet, Dr. Hutter. I made up a story, but when Officer Ryan came, I think he suspected me. That's when I made up the tale about the coats. Everyone always falls for a charity case. Except for me." She frowned. "No one wants me here." There was a knife in her hand. Where had it come from?

"What does any of this have to do with me?" It had to be that she was with Ryan. Of course that was it. She had to keep her talking. Take more minutes off the clock until he found her. She'd sent him a text right before they left the house. He had to come for her. He had to.

"You took the best one. Ryan Donavan. The guy's gorgeous. The first time I saw him walk by in his uniform my heart skipped a beat. I had to have him. I even had a date with him." She grabbed Valentina by the shoulders and shook her before storming off to pace the room. "Then you came to town."

Valentina had never looked in the eyes of a psychopath before but she was now. The woman was a lunatic. That she thought being with a law enforcement officer was going to keep her safe and secure was almost laughable. It was the reason she'd been targeted and was about to lose her life. It was a struggle to keep her wits about her and not scream like a banshee. There was no one around who would hear her pleas and it might bring a faster death. Where was Ryan? Where was Roman? Dominic? Anyone? Sweat beaded on her brow and her legs trembled. She scanned the room for anything she could use as a weapon if she was able to get her hands loose. That task looked dimmer and dimmer with every minute.

"What's with the suitcases?" Valentina nodded to the bags.

"Too much heat. I'm leaving town. Just two more to put in the car and then I'll be moving on. Well, after I kill you, that is." She took a step toward her and Valentina tried to move the chair back with her feet but it didn't work. Her brain scrambled for a reason to stall.

"The bags. You should put the rest in your car first. You wouldn't want to get blood on them." Valentina tried to dig at the tape with her finger nails and teeth when her captor wasn't looking but it wouldn't give.

"Smart." Arianne waved the knife up and down. "Yes, I'd better pack the car first. Then I can go right away. I heard you were a lawyer. Smart. Very smart." She marched over to a bag and dragged it toward the door. The wheels rolled across the floor and made a thump when she pulled it outside. Her getaway car must have been right outside when they arrived to the store. Was it stolen?

That task was repeated as she gathered the other bag and carried it out to the car. Valentina heard the sound of a trunk being shut. It might as well have been her coffin being shut as she was surely dead now. No one was coming to save her. She would die alone in some empty building. Valentina tried to move her legs but there was no give. Her wrists had to be bleeding from the stress and strain of trying to pull free.

She panted. It was hard to get air. Fear like she'd never known raced through her veins. Why had she left the safety of her father's house, or Roman's for that matter? What would Ryan do when they told him she was gone? It had been his worst fear, to care about someone only to have them lost to him. Would he ever recover? She hoped so. He deserved better.

Arianne, or whatever the hell her name was, entered the building and locked and shut the door behind her. The body has a fight or flight response in dangerous situations, and Valentina felt like the fight was over. She couldn't get loose. But the Caponelli blood that flowed through her veins said the battle wasn't over yet.

The Housewife Killer leaned down. Her face calm, her eyes blank. The woman was insane. An icy feeling traveled down Val's arm at this near death experience.

"Are you ready to die now?" Arianne's voice echoed in the quiet room.

"Not yet, bitch." Valentina jumped up, chair and all. Her head hit Arianne square in the jaw. It sent her backward to the ground and Valentina landed hard in the chair. Blood ran from the corner of Arianne's mouth and she used the back of her hand to wipe it off. The sight of it caused her to giggle.

"You will pay for that."

"I'm going to die anyway." Valentina could feel the bump starting to form on the top of her head. "What does it matter?"

"That's true. You just won't be very pretty when your boyfriend finds you."

Chapter Twenty-Three

Ryan

He'd faced a few guns pointed in his direction during his career but never had he known fear like this.

"I've got to go." He punched Roman's number into his phone as he left a confused Danny sitting at her desk. She called after him but he didn't care.

The cold chilled him to the bone as he ran to his truck. A strong north wind was nearly causing a whiteout already. He got in and the engine roared to life. He had to find her, but where was she? The others were headed to Arianne's home. It was a good chance they wouldn't fine either one there.

Ryan started driving toward her fitness center. It was the only place he could think of.

"Yeah." It was Roman. He'd forgotten that he called but he welcomed any help he could get.

"Do you know where your sister is?"

"What?"

"Valentina." He said a silent prayer that she was

safe and sound with him. "Is she with you?"

"No. Don't mince words. Tell me what's going on now," the man demanded.

"She sent me a text that she was with Arianne. That bitch is the Housewife Killer. I need to find Valentina now. I know you have surveillance everywhere, all of the time. Find her. Please." His voice trembled. They had to find her. She and Arianne had to have been together for at least an hour now. Were they too late?

The sounds of a keyboard clicking echoed over the cell. "I have a tracker on her phone. If it's with her, I should have a location in three, two, one." Roman told him the address. It was the place near the strip mall that Arianne was renting. "Dom's with me. We'll be there in one minute. I'll get back to you."

His tires skidded through an intersection. He'd gone through the only red light in town but thankfully there were no cars in sight. Everyone had hunkered down for the storm. It seemed to take forever to get there. True to his word, Roman called him back and said to meet in the back of the building where there were no windows. He noticed a car with Wisconsin plates parked out front and one with Georgia plates in the back.

He stopped his truck and took off running. Roman and Dominic were at the back door, one on each side. Each held a gun in his hands. Roman held a finger to his lips. Luckily, the door was a weak one. A swift kick and they would be in.

Ryan took Dom's place and on the count of three, Dom put a foot to the sweet spot by the doorknob and they all went rushing in. It was a sight he'd never forget. Valentina tied to a chair. Streams of black mascara ran down her cheeks. He rushed to her side. Arianne was on the floor with blood dripping from her mouth. His heart just about leapt from his chest. Not only was the love of his life alive, but she'd gotten in a few licks too. He couldn't be prouder.

"Thank god you're here," Valentina cried.

Using a knife from his belt, he cut her wrists and ankles free. She tried to stand but all the blood had rushed from her head. Ryan held her close. Her frantic heartbeat was both hurtful yet reassuring that she was alive and well.

"Are you all right, Val?" her brother asked.

"Yes, but she was going to kill me."

All eyes turned to the woman on the floor.

"No, no. It wasn't me. She's lying." With her back against the wall, Arianne got to her feet.

"She's insane." Valentina pushed out of Ryan's embrace and pointed a finger at her tormenter. "She admitted to killing all those women."

"No, I didn't." To anyone just arriving at the scene, she would be believable, but they all knew better. The lady was a psychopath and would possibly even pass a lie detector test. Those were the worst type of criminals.

"How much time do we have?" Roman asked Dominic.

The cleaner checked his phone. "They haven't even reached her house yet. The roads are getting impassable."

"Who?" Ryan asked.

"The officers sent to that bitch's house." Roman glanced around the room. For what, Ryan wasn't sure.

"You have a tracker on the police force?"

"Just the patrol cars. I like to know where they are at all times."

"Jesus, Roman." Dating Valentina was becoming a conflict of interest on many levels.

"What time is it?" Dominic made eye contact with Roman and the man nodded. What did they have planned?

"Almost time," was his response.

In a flash, Arianne lunged at Valentina, a knife in her hand. Ryan jumped in front of her. Her knife plunged into his arm. It hurt like a beast but at least Valentina was unharmed. Dominic rushed his attacker and held Arianne's arms behind her back as she screamed for him to let her go. That wasn't happening. Valentina cried and he reassured her he was just fine. In an hour or so it would be throbbing but right now adrenaline was king.

"How much longer?" Dominic directed the question to Roman.

From off in the distance, a siren wailed.

"Soon." It was the siren that started every day at one end of the town and traveled to the other announcing the noon hour. The alarm was also used the first Monday of every month in the summer for tornado drills. There was a speaker outside this building, and when it got there it would be deafening.

"Wait. We have to call this in and arrest her," Ryan said.

223

"No." The gun in Roman's hand was pointed at Arianne. The siren was close. Valentina was holding her hands over her ears. It was piercing, but the shot that rang out in the room was even louder. It happened in a second but he could see it as if in slow motion. Dom dropped his hold on the Housewife Killer and stepped back. Roman shot Arianne in the head and she crumbled to the floor. Her blood spattered on the wall behind her. Between the high winds of the storm and the earsplitting siren, it was doubtful anyone outside the building would have noticed the gunfire.

"What the hell, Roman?" Ryan grabbed Valentina and turned him toward her, as if shielding her from the violence would make everything okay.

"She was a rabid animal that had to be put down." Roman handed the gun to Dom.

"I couldn't agree more but there are laws to be followed," he argued. "You can't just shoot someone."

"You can thank me later." He winked and started giving his cleaner instructions in Italian. Then he turned back to Ryan. "Get Val out of here. Take her to my house. There will be a doctor there to see to your arm. In an hour, come back here and everything will be in place."

"What the hell?" Could he really do that?

"Just this once, do it my way." Roman locked eyes with him.

A multitude of conflicting emotions circled in his head. In the end, it was his love for Valentina that took over. She'd been a trooper but now it looked like she was about to pass out from the stress. Ryan got her out the door and safely to her brother's home where Madison was waiting with a warm blanket and hot toddy for her sister-in-law. The family's doctor stitched up his wound. After an hour, Ryan returned to the scene of the crime, but the rest of the force had beaten him to it.

The chief met him at the back door. The snow was up to his knees now, thankfully covering up all the tracks they had made before. "I was trying to reach you but with the storm the radio's been acting up."

"Yeah, it's a bad one. Did you find her?"

"She's inside." He motioned for Ryan to enter the building he'd left not too long ago.

Arianne still lay were she was, only there was a gun in her hand. If he had to guess, the medical examiner's report would probably say there was gun residue on her fingers. Roman didn't miss any detail.

Danny had her camera out. The flash almost blinded him. "Where have you been?" she asked so only he could hear. The room was abuzz with activity.

"I had to check on Valentina. I was worried when I didn't hear from her. With a nutcase on the loose, I didn't want to leave her home alone. I picked her up and drove her to her brother's place."

From the stern expression on her face it was obvious that she didn't believe him.

"How did you rip your jacket?" She waved her camera at him.

"I snagged it on a fence at their house when I slipped." He'd never lied so much as he had in the

225

last few hours. Was this what it was going to be like being involved with the Caponellis? As he glanced at the dead body, it didn't seem to matter much. It could have very easily been Valentina laying there. The killer who had stolen so many innocent lives was gone. Justice had been served.

"There's a note. Explaining why she did it. What a sick son of a bitch." Danny's words brought him back to the present.

When they had time to produce a note he didn't know and didn't care. The case was closed. The town was safe. Valentina was safe. Everything could return to normal.

"Hey, you okay, sport? You look like shit." Danny was the only one who seemed to notice he was out of sorts.

"I'm just glad it's over." He looked at the chair Valentina had been bound to just an hour before. Any hint of duct tape was now gone. Their cleaner was good. The police would sweep the place and not find a trace of the Caponellis or Dominic.

He let out a deep sigh. For the first time in weeks, he could breathe easy.

Chapter Twenty-Four

Four Months Later

Spring had come early, giving them a few seventy-degree days in March. From the look on Valentina's face when he'd given her roses for Valentine's Day the month before, he knew she'd been hoping for an engagement ring. They'd already talked about their future and that they wanted to spend it together. Even kids were discussed. That fact both excited and scared the shit out of him. She would be an amazing mother though. He knew that.

Valentina's business had boomed. Both of them. Firenza was booked all summer already for weddings. If they were going to get married, they'd have to do it on a Friday. He wanted to ask her but there was still something he had to do first. Her family was very traditional. Roman had already given his blessing but there was one more person he had to speak with first, her father, Joseph Caponelli.

He'd left early to drive to Chicago. Even though

227

he'd grown up there it had no hold over him. Everything he wanted and needed was in Lake Genoa. Roman had set up the meeting but there was still a big knot in his gut about meeting one of the most feared men in the Windy City. The one whose daughter he slept with every night. He swallowed and it lodged in his throat. He wanted the man's approval. It was important to Valentina even if she said it wasn't.

The place was like a fortress. A big iron fence laid out the border of the estate. They'd been expecting him so he was waved right in. Ryan had worn a suit. Appearances were important to the family.

It was a shock when he rang the doorbell and it was answered by Valentina's mother. They had similar looks.

"I'm Sophia. Welcome." She took his hand in hers. "It's a pleasure to finally meet you. Valentina loves you so."

"Thank you. I feel the same way. You probably know why I'm here."

"Yes. Roman told us. Follow me." Her heels echoed on the tile floor. It seemed that the woman shared the same love of shoes as her daughter. When they arrived at door, she knocked and motioned for him to go in. Sophia mouthed, "Good luck," and patted him on the shoulder.

Behind a large wood desk sat Joseph Caponelli.

"Hello, sir." Ryan approached him with his hand out but the man just motioned for him to take a seat.

"I understand you are interested in my daughter." Mr. Caponelli had a commanding voice and didn't mess around.

"Not just interested in, but in love. I am here to ask for your blessing in asking for her hand in marriage." Sure, it was the twenty-first century, but behind these walls and in their world, tradition and respect took precedence.

Joseph leaned back in his chair, the smell of leather in the air. "That I cannot give."

"Why?" Ryan's world came crashing down. He would never let anything come between them but this was going to make things so much harder.

"I don't need to give you a reason, but if you must know, you're Irish, we are Italian. You are the law, we are," he searched for a word, "on the edge of that, so to speak."

"I don't care about any of those things, only Valentina and her happiness."

"As do I, that is why I cannot allow her to marry someone whose father killed his wife."

There it was. The one thing he'd feared all his life would come back to haunt him. "I was just a kid at the time. You can't blame me for something I have nothing to do with."

"I can and I do. I'll give you one more chance, otherwise get out."

His behavior irked Ryan. So much for playing nice. The man didn't deserve such a sweet girl as his daughter. But then maybe it was just a test to see how far he was willing to go to fight for her.

"You heard about the Housewife Killer?" Ryan rested his elbows on the arms of his chair.

Joseph nodded and narrowed his eyes. "Go on."

"She took Valentina. I stepped in front of her and

took the knife that was meant for your daughter. I can show you the scar if you like." It was just a nick but it could have been much worse.

"Any man of worth would do that same thing." Joseph leaned forward in his chair. "I don't have time for this."

"Wait." Ryan thought fast. He'd rehearsed a dozen different responses but none of those would work. The man wanted something else from him. Joseph didn't want him to beg but to fight. What had Lucky Bauer said to him? Give the man something he couldn't refuse.

"I've waited long enough." Mr. Caponelli stood and so did Ryan.

"Hear me out. I was there when your son shot the Housewife Killer in the head. She was unarmed and not a threat. He shot her in cold blood."

"I don't care. The woman deserved it."

"It was against the law and he could serve time. They also covered it up. I have it all on the body camera I was wearing." The department didn't have them but hopefully the man wouldn't know that.

Joseph took a gun out of his desk and laid it on top. "So I could just shoot you now and take care of that problem myself."

"I'm smart enough to have a copy, and that copy will be made public if something happens to me. Look, I love your daughter with all my heart. I would die for her, but then she would hate you and Roman would go to prison. It's your choice. Gain a son-in-law or lose a son."

Mr. Caponelli grumbled under his breath but finally walked around the desk and held out his hand. "Welcome to the family. I'll be watching you."

Ryan exhaled for what seemed like the first time since he'd entered the office and shook his hand. He'd just lied again but it was worth it. Was this what Roman had meant when he said he could thank him later? When he got back to Genoa, he was going to find out.

Valentina

Ryan had been bursting with energy ever since he got home. He was full of surprises and he had a big one for her right now. When he showed up with a black silk blindfold, going for a ride was that last thing she thought her love had in mind. "Can I peek?" He reached for her hand before she could pull at her blindfold.

"No. Just be patient, we're almost there." They hadn't driven far, but without being able to see it seemed much longer.

The car finally slowed. The tires were on crushed rock. *Where in the world are we?*

"Now?"

"Nope." He put the car in park, turned off the engine, and got out of the car. As soon as her door opened, the scent of pine permeated the air. She wondered if they were in the forest. Ryan unbuckled her seatbelt and helped her from the car.

The blindfold was removed and her eyes

adjusted to the light. They were at Black Point, the estate they'd visited on their first date. He led her to the fountain where they'd shared a wonderful kiss. The place wasn't usually open for visitors this early in the season.

"I don't understand." It was a lovely place, but why were they there?

"This place has been here over a hundred years. I know I won't live that long, but the love I feel for you will last an eternity. When I kissed you here, I knew we were destined to be together." He got down on one knee and revealed the box he'd been hiding behind his back. Instead of the usual single solitary, there was a huge ruby surrounded by diamonds. It was perfect. "Will you make me the happiest man in the world and become my wife?"

Valentina bounced on her toes. "Yes, yes, yes."

He got to his feet and nearly hugged the air from her lungs.

She slowly slid down his body and framed his face in her hands. "And you've made me the happiest woman in the world." He kissed her again in front of the fountain. One day they would bring their children there. Maybe have a picnic on the lawn. Ryan held the ring out and she slipped it on her finger. A perfect fit, just like they were. "I love it. I couldn't have imagined anything more beautiful."

"That's what I think every time I see you," her fiancé replied. "So, my future wife. How soon do you want to get hitched?"

"The sooner the better, and I know just the right place."

They couldn't have asked for better weather on the second Friday of June. The sun sparkled on the lake. It would be a private wedding with less than fifty people at Roman Caponelli's home. Already the chairs, flowers, and crisp white runncr were in place. The guests had arrived and more would be waiting later at Firenza to join in the festivities.

Sophia fought back tears as she watched Madison adjust Valentina's veil. "My beautiful daughter."

"It's the dress. Madison, you truly have a gift." The off the shoulder straps were made of elaborate lace that also covered the bodice and parts of the A-line skirt. It was cut deep in the back where the long train was attached. The veil had been her mother's and was just as long as the train. She'd dressed underneath the gown with just as much care. Ryan would love the lace corset, thong, thigh highs, and blue garter. Her shoes were white with rhinestones but it was a good bet that he wouldn't love them as much as her red ones.

"Thanks, but it's your face that glows, not the dress."

She embraced Madison and her eyes misted. "We were blessed the day Romeo brought you into the family. You truly are a sister to me." Her mother joined in the group hug.

"Are you ready?" Stephanie poked her head in the door. "The music has started. It's time."

"Yes." Valentina dabbed at the corner of her eye

with a lace handkerchief. "I hope I don't mess up my makeup."

"You look lovely, dear." Her mother kissed her cheek and tears threatened to flow again. "Did I tell you that your father likes Ryan?"

"What?" That stopped her in her tracks. "He hates everyone."

Sophia looped her arm through Valentina's and led her from the upstairs bedroom. "He thought the man was brave and that he would do anything for you. That's all he asks from any man. Loyalty is what he respects the most. He knows Ryan will risk anything and do anything to keep you safe and love you forever." They held their skirts as they carefully took the stairs. "He hates that you will have an Irish last name though."

Valentina laughed.

"An Irishman for a son-in-law? What have you done to the family, my princess?" Her father was waiting at the bottom of the stairs. "Your beauty is only second to that of your mother's. I'm so proud of the woman you have become."

"Thank you," she choked out, and her eyes watered again. It would be a struggle to keep the tears at bay.

"No tears today. Only smiles," he said, but his eyes were glistening as well.

"It's time," Stephanie said. She was tasked with keeping everyone in line for the day. She already had Madison by the door and Arlo was there to take Sophia's arm and lead her to her seat up front. Stephanie handed Valentina the bridal bouquet of bright red roses.

Madison would be next out the door. Roman and she were the best man and matron of honor. Ryan and her brother had become very close in the last few months. Madison had designed her own dress. It was a sleeveless long, pale blue chiffon gown with a v-neckline. Music from a string quartet drifted in.

"I almost forgot." Stephanie's eyes were wide and she held an antique box in her hands. "It's from Ryan. It belonged to his mother." The box contained a simple strand of pearls. "He wanted you to have it."

It felt right to have something from his family. Everything was complete. "I love it. Can you help me put it on?"

"Let me." Joseph took the necklace from Stephanie's shaking hands before she quickly left the room. "It's perfect."

Valentina touched the pearls. How she wished his parents were here to see the man their son had become. A warmth filled her heart and as she pictured them watching from heaven.

Chapter Twenty-Five

The bridal march played. She would soon be married. Her father flipped the veil over her face and he took her arm.

When she stepped outside, it was like being in a fairytale. The sky was blue, the grass was green, and everywhere she looked a smiling face was turned her way. Danny, who she'd become good friends with, was there with a camera flashing away. As her father and she walked down the aisle, she spotted others from the police department in attendance, dressed in their uniforms. She was sure Ryan's wedding was the last place any of them ever expected to be.

Madison took her place on the opposite side of her husband. Roman winked at her. He was his usual dashing self, dressed to kill in a designer tux. But it was the man to his right that took Valentina's breath away. Officer Ryan. Her Ryan. His tux matched her brother's but he wore a red rose on his lapel while Roman's was blue.

She only had eyes for him, always for him. The

rest of the ceremony was a blur. She remembered her father placing her hand in Ryan's. Words of love and commitment were spoken by the priest but Ryan's eyes said everything she needed to hear.

Everything else was static. Valentina repeated the vows, said "I do," and gave her heart. A wedding ring was placed on her finger and she put one on his. When his lips touched hers, the fog cleared. Everything became brighter. The world was theirs for the taking.

"I now pronounce you husband and wife." Everyone got to their feet and cheered. Some boats going by tooted their horns. Ryan took her hand and they strolled down the aisle. A few people reached out and patted them on the back or arms. They stood in the entryway of Roman's house to greet everyone before heading to Firenza for the reception and dance. It didn't take long and the house was empty.

"Before we go, I have a gift for the happy couple. May I use your office, Roman?" Her father had gifts? Valentina and Ryan glanced as each other. Just giving his blessing was gift enough.

"Take a seat." Joseph ushered them in and took a seat behind the desk. The bride and groom did as he requested. "First of all," he took a key from his pocket and tossed it in front of them, "I bought you the house next door."

"What?" they both said at the same time. Every home around had to be in the millions.

"That's far too generous, sir." Ryan was having no part of that and Valentina shook her head as well.

"I knew you would say that, but hear me out. I see grandchildren on the way soon. What better place for kids to grow up than on the lake next door to their cousins? If you don't want it, then we will keep it for family members to use when they visit. Think about it, all right?"

Neither could disagree with that philosophy.

"Valentina, I'd like to speak to Ryan alone for a moment."

"Uh, okay. I will be waiting outside." She rose with a swish of her skirt. "Thank you, Father. For everything."

He waved her off and stared at her new husband.

Ryan

On the desk was a large envelope. This was serious. Had he just married the love of his life only to be ushered out the back door and killed? "I knew you lied to me about the video."

"Sir, I—" Ryan started, but was cut off.

"It doesn't matter. Anyone who has the balls to do whatever they can to get my daughter has to love her very much. This is for you." He pushed the envelope his way. "I did some checking, but don't ask where. Your father never killed your mother. He died protecting her. The man was getting too close to shutting down an organized crime family. A hit had been issued on your mother to get him to stop.

When he found out, he rushed to her side and took a bullet meant for her. The killer then shot your mother in the head. It's all on video but I wouldn't suggest viewing it. The whole thing was covered up. Your father loved her very much. I'm telling you this so you have some closure. The real case files are in the envelope." Ryan picked it up and held it to his chest. "If you want my advice, I'd let it go. Life is too short. Love my daughter, give me grandchildren, and live a long life. That is all I ask."

"Yes, sir." The packet he held contained the answers he'd wanted for so long, but did it matter anymore? He had the information he needed. There was not a murderer's blood running through his veins but a hero's. It would take time before he wanted to view what was inside. Maybe he never would. "Thank you."

"Let's join the party. All right, son?" Joseph pushed the chair back and strolled to the door.

"Yes, sir." Ryan joined him.

Valentina stood outside the door as if trying to eavesdrop. "Is everything okay?"

"It couldn't be better."

Valentina

A huge crowd greeted the happy couple as soon as they entered the door of Firenza. It was crazy that with so many family and friends wishing for a hug they made sure everyone received one. Tyler was there with his mom, not as workers but as guests. Dr. Hutter was there with his family. Ryan's coworkers were there with their dates and spouses. A lot of associates of Valentina's father were in attendance from Chicago also.

Flowers were everywhere. Stephanie had done a beautiful job with the decorating. The girl fluttered around the place like a hummingbird, making sure the bride didn't have to lift a finger. Valentina still had not gotten a word out of her about what happened the night of the Snowflake Ball when Dominic had seen her home. The man sat quietly at the bar, and whenever Valentina caught sight of him, he was following the little blonde around with his eyes. Madison's half-sister, Layla, was there and also dressed in blue. She'd danced a time or two with Arlo. Her parents danced several times as well. They had never seemed happier.

The meal had been superb. The music was lively and everyone seemed to be having a wonderful time. Their first dance as a married couple was to her favorite song, "At Last." Valentina barely had a chance to rest her feet before Steph was telling her it was time to toss the bouquet. She pressed the bouquet in her hands but the bride refused to move unless Stephanie agreed to join in the group that was hoping to catch it. The girl turned crimson when it landed in her hands.

There were a lot of hoots and hollers as Ryan removed the garter from his bride's leg and tossed it in the crowd. No one had noticed Dominic was among the crowd of single men until he raised the blue piece of lace he'd caught up in the air. The evening had been full of surprises, that was for sure.

In no time at all it was past midnight and the long day was catching up to Valentina.

"Are you ready to go, Mrs. Donavan?" Her new husband put an arm around her waist.

"Yes, Mr. Donavan."

He'd booked a room for them but she wasn't sure where. It didn't matter because as long as they were together, that was all that mattered. Tomorrow morning, she had a special surprise for him. They'd been careful, but she was pregnant. The test she'd taken that morning had been positive. Ryan never missed anything and had probably noticed her switch her champagne for water. There was no escaping Ryan, and she never wanted to.

The End

Note from the Author:

I love to write stories that take place in my home state of Wisconsin. The inspiration for the setting of this story is the beautiful tourist town of Lake Geneva. I changed the name to Genoa for the story but forgot that there is a real town called Genoa in Wisconsin. Both are beautiful places to see, so if you ever travel to Wisconsin, make sure to visit both.

When you visit Lake Geneva, be sure to take the boat ride to Black Point Estate where Ryan and Valentina went on their first date. There really are one hundred and twenty steps to get up there but it is worth it. I changed the placement of the fountain on the grounds to give them some privacy.

The speakeasy they visited is in the basement of the Maxwell House. Be sure to visit this beautiful old mansion, but make sure to get the password first.

I hope you enjoyed this Caponelli family story as there is more to come.

About the Author

Ginger Ring is an eclectic, Midwestern girl with a weakness for cheese, dark chocolate, and the Green Bay Packers. She loves reading, traveling, watching great movies, and has a quirky sense of humor. Publishing a book has been a lifelong dream of hers and she is excited to share her romantic stories with you. Her heroines are classy, sassy and in search of love and adventure. When Ginger isn't tracking down old gangster haunts or stopping at historical landmarks, you can find her on the backwaters of the Mississippi River fishing with her husband.

Facebook:
https://www.facebook.com/romancewritergingerring

Twitter:
https://twitter.com/GingerRings

Website:
http://gingerring.com/